PRAISE FOR

THE ROTTIN

In *The Rotting Whale,* Jann Eyrich artfully merges the realms of mystery and environmentalism to create an enthralling new genre: the eco-mystery. Eyrich's prose is rich, painting vivid images of both the natural and urban landscapes that serve as the backdrop for Hugo Sandoval's adventure. Readers will find themselves captivated by the offbeat hero as he ventures from the familiar streets of San Francisco to the rugged Mendocino Coast to unravel the enigma of a stranded blue whale.

The Rotting Whale is also a tale of personal growth; Eyrich delves into the complexities of Hugo's relationships with his daughter, ex-wife, and a motley crew of secondary characters. These vibrant personalities, each with their own quirks, lend depth to the story, complementing the central mystery and providing support to Hugo as he navigates the mystery.

The Rotting Whale seamlessly blends the intrigue of a classic mystery with a thought-provoking environmental theme. Jann Eyrich's eloquent writing style draws readers into the heart of San Francisco and the noir ambiance of a city on the brink of change. Readers of Dashiell Hammett's *Thin Man* Series and Louise Penny's *Chief Inspector Gamach*e Series should head to their favorite bookstore immediately.

—D.D. Black, author of *The Shadow of Pike Place,*
A Thomas Austin Crime Thriller

• • •

The Rotting Whale, the debut novel by Jann Eyrich, sparkles like the sea. Vibrant characters, an intriguing plot, and a setting with so much detail and depth you can almost taste the salty breeze.

—Janice Peacock, author of *Born to Bead Wild, A Glass Bead Mystery*

• • •

"A classic in the tradition of the best SF novelists."

— Margo Merck, Warnecke Institute

In *The Rotting Whale,* Jann Eyrich does for San Francisco and northern California in the 21st century what Armistead Maupin did in the 20th, painting a portrait of an old but vibrant and complicated city and its inhabitants as they navigate the pressing issues of our time.

Eyrich masterfully crafts mystery and intrigue from the consequences of industry and development and the high-stakes money and power at play in addressing environmental issues. A must-read for modern-day lovers of classic sleuthing and gumshoe detectives.

The Rotting Whale is an engrossing mystery that reflects the realities of our time. Eyrich leads the way toward a new and necessary integration of environmental issues into popular culture without sacrificing any of the essential elements of a great detective story.

—Ruby McConnell, author of *A Woman's Guide to the Wild*

• • •

Jann Eyrich's characters are so compelling, I would follow inspector Hugo Sandoval and his friends through any amount of coastal fog and North Coast shenanigans!

—Kathy Wollenberg, author of *Far Less*

• • •

Seeing San Francisco through Jann Eyrich's eyes in this clever eco mystery series is a great read ... we get to see the city starting to face some big changes, yet we also see an insider's guide to North Beach and the waterfront that makes you long for a crab sandwich on a foggy pier.

—Chip Conley, author of *Wisdom@Work: The Making of a Modern Elder*

• • •

Jann Eyrich has given us Hugo Sandoval, a San Francisco building inspector as a new kind of detective—he sees everything. A blue whale washes up on the beach in Mendocino and sets off a string of events that includes murder, extortion, mayhem—and a love story. Or two. Page-turning, dripping with atmosphere, a full cast of quirky supporting characters, and a bid to save the planet in a necessary new genre: the eco-mystery.

—Julia Park Tracey, author of *Veronika Layne Gets the Scoop,*
The Veronika Layne: Hot Off the Press series

A HUGO SANDOVAL ECO-MYSTERY

THE ROTTING WHALE

JANN EYRICH

AN IMPRINT OF ALL THINGS BOOK

Sibylline Press

Published in the United States by Sibylline Press,
an imprint of All Things Book LLC, California.
Sibylline Press is dedicated to publishing the
brilliant work of women authors ages 50 and older.
www.sibyllinepress.com
Distributed to the trade by Publishers Group West.

Paperback ISBN: 978-1-7367954-3-9
eBook ISBN: 978-1-960573-03-2
Library of Congress Control Number: 2023935710

Book and Cover Design: Alicia Feltman
Cover art of Mother and Baby Whale courtesy of Marina Kulik,
www.marinakulik.com. Copyright by Marina Kulik.

THE ROTTING WHALE

JANN EYRICH

Prologue

The North Coast was a lonely one. She was counting on it.

If only she could get inside the kelp bed without colliding into the rocks

If only she could reach the calm of the waters near the beach.

If only, then.

1

Hugo Sandoval, San Francisco's quixotic native son, stared out his kitchen window for reassurance. It calmed him to watch the dawn grace the little white houses of the City below, its gentle whispers of light bleeding through the fog, creating shadows on the eastern face of Russian Hill that, to him, resembled craters on the moon. He suspected it was a quietude not often found in major cities.

While the building inspector waited for the dawn to take hold, his City yawned. Hugo was familiar with her stretches; they were soft, comforting, interrupted only by a cacophony of sounds from the waterfront below where streetcars glided on slick rails, street sweepers swooshed the gutters clean, and the occasional wildlife-car-alarm barked from the sea lion's floating piers. Hugo called it City Radio, of which he was most definitely a fan, but on that October morning he was forced to tune it out. Something was gnawing at him; two somethings, in fact.

It had been a rough night for Hugo. It started with him drifting in and out of "the dream," the one where he wanders a strange, hilly, even mountainous city searching for a road to take him to—well, he never knows where. Compelled to endlessly traverse a labyrinth of streets and highways, he always awoke before reaching his destination.

After he drifted back to sleep, the insistent house phone rang from its isolation in the living room to wake him like a slap. Hugo rolled over to look at the time on his cell phone. 4:14 a.m. The ringing stopped before he could throw back the bedding. *No one calls on the house phone*, he thought, fighting for a few more minutes of sleep, *except*—. Hugo's cell phone started to buzz. He grabbed it in time, but the connection was weak and broke off. The phone buzzed again, and again failed to connect. The caller ID said *A*, A for Ava, his daughter. Since she had left the City for a remote marine research center up the coast, Ava was often out of range. Hugo was happy her career had taken off, but the distance had put a strain on the father-daughter relationship. The fact that Ava hadn't called in weeks, and now, these pre-dawn attempts to connect left Hugo anxious and wide awake.

For the past sixteen months, Hugo had been the sole occupant of the top floor of an Italianate duplex perched at the north end of Grant Avenue. The spacious flat overlooking the waterfront was vintage San Francisco, but it was not his. Since his divorce Hugo had been house-sitting for an old friend, an esteemed professor emeritus at the Art Institute, Jean-Michele Moreau, JM. The professor had conveniently flown to Paris for an indefinite exile; *an escape*, he told friends. The night before his departure, JM and Hugo had traded stories at Specs' Bar where the artist confided more than a few truths over brandies. JM began with confessions of his own marital disasters before advising Hugo on his recent painful separation.

"Win her back, son," advised the older Bohemian as he handed Hugo the keys to his flat. "Carmen is a rare work of art; *formidable*."

In his brief residency on the top floor of 2101 Grant Avenue, Hugo had pored through first editions of *Howl* and stacks of *City Lights Journals*; he listened with reverence to the rare, personalized pressing of 'Thelonious Alone In San Francisco' on the flat's vintage turntable. He wrote poetry at the kitchen table and, thanks to JM's vintage candy-apple-red espresso machine, Hugo had renewed his love affair with the thick dark liquid. Although the scene had flared before his time, Hugo was content knowing that his own exile was framed in the art and artifacts of the Beat Generation, a culture that once defined his City.

It was a solemn Hugo who stood at the kitchen balcony sipping his double espresso with a clumsy mark of steamed milk that defined the macchiato; solemn and worried. He knew Ava's work on the coast put her at risk from time to time—just last summer she and her team tracked a humpback whale entangled by fishing gear for two days until they were able to cut it free. He hated the risks she took, but he trusted her. His macchiato had gone cold. *Why was Ava trying to reach him at 4 am?*

In the garden below, Mrs. Tsantis, the attractive proprietress of the North by South Greek Deli retrieved her Pomeranian from the rose bed. As was her nature, the neighborhood's Greek siren casually allowed her dressing gown to slip off her shoulders. Hugo barely took notice that morning; instead, he closed his eyes and looked out over the Bay, inhaling deeply to drink in the tide on its retreat. The lingering breath of the Bay's muddied shore reminded him he needed a shower. Before jumping in, he redialed his daughter's cell phone, to no avail, and left another message with her office at the marine lab.

Hugo loved Jean-Michele's shower with the floor-to-ceiling white subway tiles and the extravagant water pressure, which inspired some of his best thinking. It was a luxury, indeed an indulgence for a single man such as he. While his body longed to linger under the waterfall, he cut his shower short, but not before the hot water revealed what had triggered his recurring dream in the pre-dawn hours.

It was as he feared, the fallout that awaited him on Pier 50 was *not* the culprit; no, the trigger was far more intimate and disturbing, especially now with Ava in the mix.

Repeated texts had knocked Hugo's cell phone to the floor.

Ping.

Their insistence bounced the inspector's phone along the slippery linoleum out of reach. When he finally snagged it, wet feet squealing, he read,

sorry dad. out of range. come see my whale. need you

He quickly texted back,

where r u?

In the fall of 2011 Hugo was still a fan of the phone call. For him, the person-to-person touch was everything. Texts left him cold. What little he did know about texting he had learned from a teenage Ava on their explorations around the City. They were quite the team. He would show her where a decorative Victorian cornice extended far over the next building's façade, and she would demonstrate the art of texting while sharing a stack of banana pancakes at Mama's on Washington Square.

Hugo stared at his hand hoping for any reply from his girl.

Nothing. No response to his text. He retreated to the bedroom to dress.

It was not unusual for Hugo to be called upon to resolve issues outside the normal routine of a building inspector. Colleagues respected his impassioned methodology and admired his calm, professional demeanor as he sorted out puzzles of all shapes and sizes. In the course of his duties as a building inspector, Hugo might be found facing off a slumlord or a corrupt politician, but he tackled more modest, more personal projects with the same dedication. These often yielded triumphs that seared him to the heart of the public. When the headlines demanded comment, Hugo's standard reply was, "It's all part of the job." At least his interpretation of the job.

What the public failed to see was how Hugo thrived on untangling the labyrinth of City regulations that had long hog-tied its citizens. That passion prompted his ex-wife Carmen to call the City *Hugo's mistress.* As the years had unfolded, Hugo allowed his work to consume him, often pushing his marriage to the sidelines. What had been a good partnership fell apart.

Until the morning of the missed calls, Hugo had always been eager to take on new challenges, but this time it was different. This time, it was attached to a face he loved. As he contemplated the steamed milk glued to the sides of his favorite mug, Hugo wondered if it was time to call the woman JM had branded as his *formidable ex.* But why alarm her with the facts? Even with his ego aside, he wasn't sure Carmen was the call he needed to make.

While the early morning light forced its way through the leaded glass of the flat's front door, he hesitated before going through. Perhaps it was to settle his Borsalino or straighten the crisp white cuffs of his shirt that had crept outside the sleeves of his trademark leather jacket, but whatever the reason, Hugo was caught off guard by his own reflection. In the glass of the hall tree, he saw the shadow of his father, had his father lived into his fifties.

"*Tranquilo,*" he whispered. It was time to call Harrison.

Crossing the threshold, the worried father punched *H* on his speed dial.

2

Owner and sole operative of Brick + Mortar Investigations, T. Ray Harrison answered the early hour call as if he were in his office on Folsom Street, despite waking at his home on the Mendocino Coast. The investigator hadn't picked up his mail in the City in more than three weeks but, on duty or not, a dawn call deserved his full attention. Especially if the caller was Hugo.

Sandoval was a mess, thought T. Ray when Hugo woke him from a deep sleep. As the building inspector's best friend and confidante, T. Ray knew the divorce had taken a toll on the normally resilient inspector and expected he was about to hear yet another perspective on the split from the lonely bachelor.

Thelonious Raymond Harrison, III, lived 200 miles north of the City on the edge of the Mendocino National Forest. He settled peacefully off the grid with his wife, Daisy, in their hand-crafted house, which was a homage to his roots. Marguerite "Daisy" Harrison was a singer with Jimmy Buffet's Coal Reefer Band when she met T. Ray in Key West. It was more than her voice and her moves on stage that made T. Ray stalk the tour. They married while on the road, just outside Cincinnati.

Although his own wife would argue the point, T. Ray was certain it was more than the convergence of Hugo turning fifty, Carmen leaving him, and their only child flying the nest that had rocked Hugo's world. No, T. Ray insisted, it was the City itself that was tearing at the core of his friend.

Sandoval was a mess was the mantra ringing in his ears when he answered the phone. T. Ray thought through it again as his burly frame moved quietly from the bedroom to allow his wife to burrow back down in the sheets. As T. Ray stretched, his whole body embraced the redwood and pine forest that surrounded their home. Through a gap in the woodland canopy, he watched a planet chase the moon toward the horizon. *A gutsy move; probably Mars.*

On the phone, Sandoval sounded panicked to T. Ray. "Slow down, Chief—is she hurt?" T. Ray's voice was deliberately calm.

"I don't know. I don't think so." Until that second, it hadn't occurred to Hugo that Ava could be hurt.

"Forget I said that. I'm sure she's fine," T. Ray said, his tone slowing and softening. "Just tell me exactly what she said,"

He pulled on his pants as he listened patiently to Hugo's report of the pre-dawn messages. While his friend read the messages over again, T. Ray fumbled in the dark for the head-hole in his faded midnight blue hoodie, the one that read, *Party like it's 1491.* The shirt had been a gift from a grateful Pomo elder for tracking a lost child of the tribe and seemed fitting for the morning.

"Ava's voice kept breaking up. I could only catch pieces of her words, '*I parked—Cloud—cliff—looking down on the whale,*'" Hugo repeated.

"That's it?"

"No. A few minutes later she called back, or tried to," Hugo went on. "Before the connection broke again, I heard distinctly, *red tag—beach house—*"

"That's it, then." T. Ray tried to piece the words together "That's all of it?"

"No, stay with me here," Hugo said. "She must have known her calls weren't getting through and turned to texting."

After listening carefully to the fragmented texts, T. Ray paused. "Sandoval, the last text, read it to me again."

"rancher oks me to park on his land. big job ahead. need you here," repeated Hugo reading the text. Hugo let that final message sit for a minute. Finally, he muttered, "She's never said that to me before."

"What, that she needs you? Hugo, I'm sure she's fine," said T. Ray. Immediately T. Ray knew he had made a mistake—called his old friend by his first name—a gaffe he instantly regretted. It just was not done, not between them, anyway. Despite T. Ray's casual reassurance, the concerned father knew that Harrison was worried as well.

"Look, *Sandoval*," T. Ray spoke with authority to calm his friend. "I think I know the ranch she's talking about. I'll call you when I find her."

Hugo wanted to be there for his girl, not send the cavalry. "She called me not you, *Harrison*."

"All right, then; get on up here. Leave the City right now. Meet me in Noyo Harbor at the Blue Crab Shack. It's going to take you three hours, the way you drive that old piece of shit—does it even run?"

"Harrison. I can't leave the City this morning, not just yet. I have a meeting in the Port in—," he looked at his watch. "In forty-two minutes."

"Skip it," said T. Ray, taking an easy shot from the cheap seats, although he knew the stakes.

"I was the one who called the meeting; I can't bail. You know it took me months to pull this together. If I back out now," he paused, his voice dropping, "God knows what she'll think." Hugo cut himself off.

"You lost me—who, the mayor? Since when are you worried about what she's going to think?" Now it was T. Ray's turn to pause. "Sandoval, you still there? This meeting is about Pier 50, right?" T. Ray sounded almost hurt. "Why didn't you tell me the field trip was today? I would have come down. This *is* huge. After all these years of fighting over jurisdiction, how did you ever get them to agree to show up? Sandoval?"

T. Ray checked his phone to see if they were still connected. He wanted to goad Hugo into talking, not an easy task.

"Let's play who's who. Who is on your guest list? The State Lands Commission, of course; the BCDC, naturally; don't forget the gang from the Port, hey! What would we do without those guys?"

"Harrison, not today."

"Just getting them to show up is amazing, don't get me wrong—and at low tide! Hold on, I think I'm missing someone, a key player. Sandoval, help me out," T. Ray teased.

"The developers," Hugo murmured.

"Ah, so it's not the mayor, it's the *developer's attorney* you're wanting to impress. It's their hired gun, the charming and brilliant Carmen Sandoval, mother of your only child, *well, the only one we know of.* Carmen is coming to the show. Is that why you didn't call me into town?"

"'Nuf," Hugo protested, but failed to stop the deluge.

"Your Carmen will be promoting *her* clients who plan to turn Pier 50 into a corporate mecca, or are they thinking more of a playland reserved for members only?" T. Ray added with a tinge of sympathy, "I feel your pain, brother. I do."

Hugo grunted.

"What *is* your plan, Chief? Squeeze them all into a boat, cruise underneath the pier and then what, hope the tide comes in and drowns the lot of 'em?" T. Ray chuckled. "In my opinion, they deserve to get wet at the very least. When I think of how many years these same officials have danced around this issue of jurisdiction while taking the City's Port tenants for a ride, I'm just sayin' it would be poetic justice, Sandoval. That's all." He chuckled to lighten the mood as he climbed into his battered forest green 1949 Chevrolet pickup.

T. Ray goosed, "I have money down at the office you don't even get into the boat. It's nothing personal, mind you."

Hugo didn't take the bait. Although there was an outside chance the forest had devoured their connection, the silence on the other end of the line was the type of silence endemic to his friend, the kind of silence that let T. Ray know Hugo had drifted off the page.

"*Damn it,* she knows better," Hugo muttered, loud enough for T. Ray to hear.

"I take it we're back to Ava now. Look, Sandoval, we need to talk fast. Run it by me again 'cuz I'm going to lose you in a few turns," T. Ray warned as he guided the Chevy down the old logging road towards the coast.

Still no response.

"Sounds to me like your Ava just needs a Dad visit, Sandoval. Look, I'll call you the minute I put my eyes on the girl," he added.

Hugo responded with a musical yet vaguely guttural grunt.

T. Ray knew that grunt well. The inspector was working out a problem. Typically, those grunts were followed by an impenetrable silence. Upon reflection, T. Ray knew better than to jump in with both feet instead of waiting out the silence; but waiting just wasn't his style.

He would later confess to his wife, "Holy Mother, I couldn't help it. Daisy, you know how stubborn he gets. I just rambled on and on about the hundreds of illegal dwellings on the coast, about how some outbuildings are completely abandoned while some even have squatters; hell, old ranches are thick with them. Those stories are always making the papers; you know that, honey."

T. Ray could feel Daisy holding her tongue as she waited for him to circle back around. "*Cheez,* I couldn't shut up about it. Thank god I drove out of range."

Although the temperature was in the forties, the Chevy's old engine turned over like a charm. For luck, T. Ray lovingly patted the sacred dashboard strewn with shells, beach sticks and a plastic hula girl and coasted down to the backwater road. He steered the cantankerous pickup past the split in the road where a burned-out redwood stump stood in defiance, past forest floors bedded thick with ferns, wild iris, and trillium. Nearing the coast, he cracked the window to breathe in the marine layer with its intoxicating smell of the Pacific, but the elixir failed to soothe his guilt. He knew his friend had hung up more worried than when he had first called for help.

"Fair enough," T. Ray exhaled; but he was worried, too.

It was a simple thing. Ava Rose Sandoval, his best friend's headstrong daughter, had dropped a name in the fragmented pre-dawn conversation with her father. It was the name of the ranch, the one on which she was invited to park her Airstream.

It was that name that gave her Uncle T. pause. *Dillon.*

3

As a child of rootless immigrants, Hugo defined his own roots as a first-generation American. A proud native son of San Francisco, he was born in the Basque Belt, the border between North Beach and Chinatown where his mother had settled from Spain. Hugo was also his Cuban father's son. The color of his skin and how he came to be, he insisted, was irrelevant to his work. So armed, Hugo took on his job with unrivaled dedication, earning respect and devotion one permit at a time. For more than three decades, the people of the City and County of San Francisco had put their trust in the simple building inspector many reverently called their Watchdog. Although his battles in a city that was always reinventing did not always make the news, word got out that the City had a defender against unrestrained development, someone they could trust, one of their own.

With little warning, the development tide suddenly turned. From a citizenry devoted to reclaiming its historic shoreline, Hugo saw a shift to one that embraced development. City Hall opened the floodgates to an aggressive breed of investors determined to reshape the waterfront and create an overwhelmingly vertical downtown. The transformation made headlines. Not only was the San Francisco skyline being redrawn, but as Hugo watched helplessly, neighborhood after neighborhood had become threatened with gentrification—the Mission District, the Excelsior, even his beloved North Beach. It was as if public hostility toward skyscrapers and carpetbaggers had been taken out with the trash.

As early as 2005, the seasoned building inspector cautioned the City that a downtown tower project proposed near the waterfront would be precariously perched on unstable landfill. Despite his efforts, his warning was shelved. Hugo believed he was watching his City disappear in real time, broken up and sold to the highest bidder. In 2009 he took a leave of absence from his office in the near-sighted DBI, the City's perpetually tarnished Department of Building Inspections. No one begged him to stay.

Hugo found himself isolated, hog-tied by the constraints of the confidentiality clause in his contract. He was not a happy man and, in the months that passed in exile, he grew increasingly restless and depressed. In early 2010, when contacted for an interview about sea level rise and its impact on downtown development he decided to break ranks. In his interview with Editor Horton of *The Weekly*, Hugo's comments defiantly outlined the fragility of the natural shoreline of San Francisco:

> *"Our entire waterfront is built on an estuary. In effect, we are building on water anchored only to bedrock far below sea level," stated DBI's former Chief Building Inspector Hugo Sandoval. "When the ground sinks and the sea level rises, high tides and storms will have their heyday, joining with the Bay itself in reclaiming its natural wetlands. Imagine leveling sand dunes and dredging shoals to create real estate. Crazy, right? But that's exactly what we did. We have been destroying those natural barriers that protected our shoreline for decades. Regardless of who set this in motion, it's time we all owned it."*

Hugo's brief "retirement" had brought a latent acrophobia to the surface. His fear of heights flared after a traumatic inspection. Intensive tests determined that there was a limit as to how high Hugo could go without passing out. The DBI had no choice but to recognize that Hugo's condition severely limited his professional capacity to inspect buildings over five floors high.

The politically savvy mayor-elect recognized an opportunity when she saw one. After reading the sea-level rise article in *The Weekly*, the mayor realized by creating a new job at DBI, her office could offer Hugo a title he couldn't possibly refuse: Special Inspector for Port Projects. The new position would keep him on the ground for a few years—at least until the towers went up—preserve his pension, and by answering only to the mayor's office, give former Chief Sandoval freedom from the DBI and the Port. Along with the impressive title, the job came with an elusive hall pass—full access to all waterfront projects.

Advisors close to the mayor suspected the waterfront was exactly where Hugo wanted to make his stand. It was a good move on the mayor's part, with the waterfront being on the front lines of social and environmental justice issues, especially with climate change increasingly forcing her hand. Shouldering up to the unflappable building inspector would prove to be an invaluable asset when pushed turned to shove.

Intrigued by the challenge and cheered on by Carmen, who had found his wallowing both unhealthy and tedious, Hugo decided to give the city another go.

As Special Inspector for Port Projects, his first six months had proven bumpy. Carmen left him, then Ava took a job with a new marine research center on the North Coast, despite both her parents reminding her that whales were often spotted inside the Golden Gate. It had been a long fourteen months for Hugo since his family had broken apart. In the quiet, he focused on projects like the confrontation on Pier 50 which now loomed in front of him, its shape no less threatening than the iconic Transamerica Pyramid, its obelisk piercing the fog.

Riding his trusty mustard-yellow Gitane 10-speed, Hugo traversed the broken Embarcadero to the pier where he and others would gather to inspect the embattled shoreline of San Francisco. His route would trace the City's fragile seawall from Pier 23 south, cruise beneath the Bay Bridge, then one by one pass the even-numbered piers to the crossing of the Mission Creek Channel where the Third Street drawbridge would take him to his destination at Pier 50. Designed by Joseph Strauss of Golden Gate Bridge fame, the 143-foot landmark bridge had been renamed the Lefty O'Doul Bridge in 1969. It was far and away Hugo's favorite bridge in the City. He even kept a photo of its 1933 ribbon cutting on his desk at Otis Street, next to the one of Ava receiving her master's in marine science at UC San Diego.

Traffic was light along the Embarcadero at that early hour. Hugo enjoyed pedaling hard along the rim of the City, skirting the Rincon, cruising under the Bay Bridge, only to slow down at Pier 30. Perched on the pier was Red's Java House, a favorite hangout of Hugo's. The historic outpost with its genuine waterfront dive vibe spoke to him and with hunger gnawing at his insides, he was tempted to grab a quick dog for breakfast, even snag the latest edition of *The Weekly*, but he knew the low tide wouldn't wait.

Barely a mile south of the Bay Bridge, the yellow Gitane and its rider waited at a red light at King and Third Streets for the streetcar to pass in front of the Giant's ballpark. When its conductor clanged the bell in salute to the chief, Hugo reluctantly waved back. Despite being invigorated by the morning ride, he fought the impulse to run. The building inspector had reached his tipping point.

Like the wanderer in his dream, he was lost.

4

THERE WAS NO CHOP THAT MORNING, not even a ripple on the Bay. It was quiet on the water; so quiet he thought he could hear the tide returning.

Thank god, Hugo sighed inwardly. He pushed down his aquaphobia and calmed his racing heartbeat as he boarded the outboard. By his count the boat was overloaded but Hugo had total confidence in the pilot of the small but stealthy craft, a 21-foot Boston Whaler. Fire Captain Wayne Tiao, a classmate of Hugo's from Galileo High School, had been the commander of his department's famous maritime unit the *Phoenix*, the little fireboat credited with saving the City's Marina District from the fires following the 1989 Loma Prieta earthquake. Twenty-two years later, the captain showed off his expertise on the water by weaving the boat through a menagerie of pier footings that honeycombed the City's southern shoreline. Tiao glanced at Hugo who, despite being braced against his shoulder, had a grip on the whaler's console like a goose barnacle attached to a rock.

"Chief, I'm going to swing around that marker and drift in under the deck with the current; piece of cake," the captain assured his old friend.

While the other passengers resisted the cold, Hugo sent his

tongue to test the bay's seasoned breath, a puree of diesel boat gas, thickened by bait fish churned up in the wake of a passing ferry, then generously salted.

From the waterline, the City that morning appeared to be in mourning with the somber residue of fog backing away from the shoreline, like distant relatives. Hugo felt himself comforted by familiar landmarks he was seeing as if for the first time from sea level. Captain Tiao turned the boat towards Pier 50. With the eight-mile span of the Bay Bridge at his back, Hugo reverently watched his City rise with the ascent of the dawn; street by street, its rooftops ignited by the russet-yellow sun.

Captain Tiao gently guided the double-hulled boat through a colonnade of moss-draped pier posts toward the seawall, the shoreline's ultimate defender. It was a rare minus tide, which allowed the boatload of officials to literally float beneath the aging pier to breach what had been the "new" shoreline of nineteenth-century San Francisco. Hugo had tears in his eyes as the whaler closed in on the scarred and sacred place in the City's history.

"We're looking at the second seawall," Tiao shouted to his passengers over the low purr of the outboard, "Sections of the earlier seawalls were built by sinking ships abandoned at the end of the Gold Rush."

"Not whaling ships?" mused the lead engineer from the Port of San Francisco, Mike Shrek, a bitter émigré from the New Jersey shore. Hugo thought Shrek appeared oddly uncomfortable with what was leaking from the corroded pipes that dangled from the pier above their heads.

"Hard to say. No whalers in this section that I know of although this shoreline was a huge whaling port in the late 1800s," Tiao said with reverence. "It was a saltmarsh land grab that went on for years. Fill came from everywhere—even debris from the 1906 earthquake ended up in these seawalls," Tiao added.

At the bow of the modern whaler rode Ben Strauss, the

representative from the BCDC, the conservation agency for the communities around the bay. As he snapped photos of the seedy underside of Pier 50 to document any signs of life, the boat slightly rocked. Drifting deep under the pier Hugo gripped the console even tighter when Strauss struggled to capture a fern rooted in moss clinging to a post as it reached for the light.

Across from Shrek, the presumptive developer's architect scribbled notes in his slick all-weather expedition journal. The international firm specialized in waterfront land use but until that morning ride, the architect admitted, "I've never actually been *under* one of our projects."

Like her companions, the eager emissary from City Hall, Celia Winslow, wore a life vest and hard hat; unlike her companions, Hugo observed, it made her even more attractive.

Hugo had respectfully declined the hardhat, choosing instead to put his faith into the inward security and outward grit of his Borsalino he had purchased at Billy's Junk Shop in North Beach just weeks before the quake in '89. Back then, it was *rookie* Inspector Sandoval who had been dispatched to investigate the latest complaint from tenants living above Billy's counter-culture junk shop on Grant Avenue. The complainant claimed the junk shop's owner kept exotic snakes and allowed them to roam the store after hours. According to the tenants in the floors above, one of the anacondas had been haunting the old building, turning up in hallways and flats unannounced.

Celia gracefully made her way to the console for a chat. "I just love your fedora," she gushed to Hugo. "It's vintage, isn't it?"

Hugo had suspected Celia had a crush on him since the mayor's Christmas party.

"It's old if that's what you mean. Technically, it's a *Borsalino* fedora," He replied a little coldly, not to encourage her.

"I read that you are, well, let's just say, 'uncomfortable' on the water. I must say, Inspector, conquering your fear in the line of duty this morning is most admirable." Celia smiled up at him. "And how interesting that you chose the Port as your specialty."

Hugo glanced at Tiao, who cared little for hats or barefoot sirens.

"Better sit down now, Ms. Winslow," Tiao said. "It's a little risky under here." He handed his old chum the searchlight.

Hugo was certain he saw the captain fight back a smile as Celia moved forward. She called from her seat, "Dear Inspector, exactly what are we looking for?" Her voice echoed underneath the rotting pier.

Hugo thought the echo gave the ride a Fun House feel. To answer, he trained the light on the dripping pipes that serviced the café above. Much like his inspection of Billy's Junk Shop twenty years before, the aging undercarriage of Pier 50 proved unremarkable. It was clear that the sewer lines servicing the Two Bits Bar + Café topside would need to be removed and rerouted but, sadly, years of draining city runoff and wastewater from the waterfront joint into the Bay had taken its toll. What had once been a thriving tidepool was now a dead zone.

Suddenly Hugo landed the searchlight on an intriguing section of crumbling rip rap. Tiao gently kicked the engine into reverse to slow the boat. The beam of light revealed the unmistakable tip of a rust-encrusted ship's anchor reaching out from under the crumbling seawall like hands through prison bars.

"Wayne, can you get closer?" asked Hugo excitedly and tossed his cell phone on the console before moving forward.

"Tide's coming in, Chief," Tiao said. "Go for it but make it snappy." Tiao pulled in close enough for Hugo to lean far beyond the bow of the whaler and touch the anchor. Hugo felt a pain in his chest and pulled back. The whaler's hull was scraping the rocks.

"Shrek—grab my belt, will you?"

Strauss set his camera to document the discovery in low light as Hugo stretched his body over the blackish water. With each reach, Hugo was blasted with the gas from the decomposing organisms that somehow survived in the contaminated sea water. Fighting off the nausea, he shouted, "Hold steady, Wayne!" and reached forward again.

Architect Weston, safely seated against the console, kept a worried eye on the looming pier structure above. "Don't stand up, Chief. Hang on!"

Hugo's right hand clawed at something stuck in the wall while his left braced the boat against the rusted leaves of the mammoth anchor chain. When Shrek pulled him back into the whaler, Hugo's hand was dripping blood.

Celia gasped. "You're bleeding! Where's the first aid kit, Captain?"

"Don't rinse your hand until we test it, Chief!" Weston shouted. He was the only one who laughed.

The tide was coming in fast and, seeing they were running out of headspace, Tiao quickly put the engine in reverse and backed out from under the pier.

Hugo ducked his way back to the console holding his fist to the side to keep the blood from dripping on the deck. When Tiao gave Hugo a handkerchief, he caught his old friend transferring an object into his pocket, something clawed free from the seawall.

Ben Strauss switched to video as the whaler glided free of the colonnade of concrete pier posts. Hugo noticed how each post was unique with its own sculpture garden of green moss, salt-stained watermarks, and rusted bolt heads grasping rotted weathered cross beams.

"Ben, do you think you could send me those photos?"

Tiao triumphantly returned the grand tour to the landing against a Philip Glass symphony of gull's cries, underscored by the low sputtering of the whaler's outboard. As the officials climbed off the boat, the chorus of arguments about which agency was on the hook for repairs rose before the passengers ascended to Pier 50's dock.

"I thought they would sort it out," Hugo was dismayed.

With his riders safely on the pier, Tiao shrugged. "Well, you tried. Proud to have you on board, Chief Inspector."

"*Former* Chief Inspector," Hugo corrected. "Many thanks for the tour, Wayne."

"Let's see that hand," Tiao reached for his first aid kit.

"It's nothing," Hugo said, although he was happy to let the firefighter clean it up.

Tiao taped the gauze up tightly. "Okay, now let's see the other hand," he said, smiling.

Hugo pulled a small blue bottle out of his pocket caked in silt and held it for the captain to see.

"I'll be damned. Easily 19th century. What do you think, from a ship, maybe a labor camp?"

"Hard to say. It was deep in there, but that wall is breaking apart and let me have it."

"You know Hugo, until you lunged for that seawall, I had forgotten that your dad worked these docks."

Hugo had not forgotten. He could never forget. His father's death on the waterfront was always in the back of his mind. The morning's ride in the whaler, not to mention actually touching the seawall made his father seem very close. Hugo's had been a colorful childhood, full of ferry boat rides and fishing trips on the Bay until the day his father didn't come home from work.

"Hugo, your phone,"

As he climbed the gangplank, Hugo's hand, taped and re-wrapped in a clean handkerchief throbbed. With the other hand Hugo fumbled for his flip phone where a message from T. Ray awaited.

Have lead on whale, get up here!

5

A BLAZING FIREPIT AWAITED on the large deck over the Bay where members of the expedition joined their support staffs and other officials eager to tell tales of their adventure under the pier. A small, athletic, middle-aged woman in bike shorts filled their coffee mugs without consideration for the biting cold. Toni, the sassy Sicilian import along with her business partner owned and operated the popular waterfront establishment whose pipes leaking into the Bay had triggered all the attention.

Balking at joining the crowd, Hugo chose instead to drift to the far rail. He saw her coming through the firepit crowd and other joggers, bikers and seagull-feeders at the pier. He wasn't prepared to speak with her and there had been times when he doubted he could ever face her again, but there she was; facing her was part of his job. Fourteen months since the last time he'd seen her, she was as beautiful as the day they'd met, Nevertheless, she was incoming—the sandy-haired Brit with a sharp wit and curvaceous form, the mother of his daughter—Carmen Knights-Day Sandoval.

Daunted by his emotions, especially after the morning he'd already had, Hugo defaulted to his comfort zone, talking shop.

"See how small their kitchen is?" Hugo opened, nodding to the wing of the Two Bits Bar + Café behind her. "It's part of the original building. When the Port wanted to extend cargo out on the pier, they cut the warehouse in two and ran rails right out to the end of this dock. Completely destroyed the look of the bulkhead," he shook his head. "Mission Revival style," he stopped mid-sentence.

"Hello yourself, Hugo," Carmen said.

What sort of British bluebloods name their daughter Carmen? Hugo wondered. "How are your parents, by the way?" The topic seemed safe enough.

"Very well, and they send their love. You should call them." With an all-too-familiar look, Carmen weighed the figure before her. "You're wet," her eyebrows raised, "and you're hurt," she pronounced after her initial inspection. "Whatever possessed you to throw this charade in the first place, Hugo?"

"For starters, it's my job." He debated asking her about Ava.

With her coffee pot empty, Toni, the deceivingly petite import from Lower Manhattan's Hell's Kitchen, swooped by, ignoring Carmen, preferring to dote on Hugo. "Chief, go sit at the bar. I'm putting up a plate for you. Teri will get you anything else you need, *on the house, of course*," she whispered to Hugo before hustling back to the kitchen.

"This is new. You're taking bribes now, Hugo. Oh, splendid. Well done." Carmen jabbed at her ex with a smile on her face.

Just then, a local TV news anchor rushed out of the cafe to the deck, crew in tow. Tina Vaughn, overdressed for an expedition to the waterfront, nodded in Hugo's direction before flashing what Carmen interpreted as a seductive smile before dragging her news team to the firepit. The not-too-subtle look piqued Carmen's interest. She had already observed Celia Winslow smiling in their direction for what seemed like an uncomfortable amount of time.

"Hugo, I'm only curious, mind you, but how is it that all the women on this dock—"

"Pier, Carmen, it's a *pier*."

"—all the women on this *pier* appear to be, I don't know, what should we call it, *intimately* drawn to you?" Carmen shot across the bow, her confident smile fading.

While Hugo had always enjoyed the sparring, he mostly enjoyed looking at his ex-wife; it had been a long time. They had been in love, wildly in love, the three of them—Carmen, Hugo, and his City, until Carmen kicked the City to the curb and went off to law school. In any event, that was *his* explanation as to why they split.

Carmen Knights-Day Sandoval was exactly what society photographers were looking for in a fifty-something female political figure. Wrapped in a calm, albeit cryptic, veneer, her presence at any event gave the assembly a little class, the level of class San Franciscans always enjoyed. A leading columnist for the San Francisco daily had labeled a young Carmen "The Rock Rose." That nickname had captured her style as then-director of Environmental Health for the City and County of San Francisco. To all concerned, she could be hard as a rock, at the same time beautiful as a rose. Through multiple administrations, a parade of mayors had relied on her lightning-quick and decisive management style, which kept her staff in top form and her associates gasping for air. When Carmen jumped the bureaucratic ship for law school ten years before, she had left both the City and her husband adrift.

"Honestly Hugo, you set up this ridiculous meeting for what purpose? My dear man, you cannot save them all. Sadly, it is over for these courageous women; it's been over for some time. Be kind to them and all of us and stop dragging this out."

"It's not my call, Carmen. I'm only the eyes and ears for the mayor." Hugo spit out the bait.

"No, dear," quipped Carmen, "that's *her* job," nodded to Celia, who was enjoying her moment on camera.

The newscaster signaled to Hugo from across the pier, but he waved her off. He couldn't clear his head. Carmen was in the way. In fact, she closed in tight.

"I know your face," she declared as she scrutinized her ex-husband. "You saw something, didn't you?" She enjoyed how his mouth clenched and his cheeks flexed when he met her gaze. "What's down there, Hugo?" she whispered.

It used to bother her when he wouldn't answer. He was never rude exactly, just Hugo, which would prompt Carmen to explain to Ava that it was the way her father sorted out things in head. But was it just an excuse? As a little gust off the Bay made Carmen turn her head away, she realized after walking out on him, she wasn't his confidante anymore.

"Why don't I give you a ride back to Otis Street and you can fill me in?" Carmen broke the standoff. Hugo hesitated but she cut him off, "Right then. Away with you to your illicit breakfast, I have calls to make. Meet me in the car when you're ready." She took two steps back to allow the news crew to engulf the floundering Hugo.

"Inspector, who is responsible for the deteriorating infrastructure of Pier 50? Is it the City?" asked Tina Vaughn, pushing her microphone in front of his face.

Hugo had always been a wild card on camera. The press could never be certain who would show up. Would it be the thoughtful and reserved public servant or the clever and opinionated people's advocate—or both?

"Tina, it all comes down to jurisdiction. Officially, the Port maintains a fifty-foot setback from the edge of the Bay, but the precise location of the shoreline is contested. Where does it stop and start? Case in point, you and I are standing on a historic pier that straddles not one *but two* seawalls."

"Inspector Sandoval, but who is on the hook for the repairs?" The news anchor closed in, flashing her on-camera smile for her prey.

"The City has a clear, contractual responsibility to their Port tenants to maintain leaseholds like this café but historically the costs would be passed onto the tenants but that's not what's on the table today."

"Could you expand on that?"

Hugo tried to back away from the camera but strong winds off the Bay spun the inspector about like a sail.

"It's critical mass," he said, shielding the reporter. "What is decided today about Pier 50 will impact the development of all the piers but unless the City demands that future developments ensure protection against sea-level rise, it's game over. Who is going to strengthen the seawalls or restore our historic piers like this one? It's our *legacy* we've put out for bid."

The Sicilian in bike shorts cut in front of the camera allowing Hugo to make his escape. "Your breakfast is getting cold," she whispered over her shoulder.

He was grateful for the distraction and secretly hoped she remembered the sausages he liked.

"You recording? Look, it's amazingly simple," explained the club owner, putting her spin on the morning. "The cost of these repairs will put us out of business, period, end of story—which is exactly what the Port wants. My partner and I are one of just three women tenants on the Port properties. *Three* out of hundreds of leases! The Port has been trying to get rid of us for years so they can turn the lot over to big developers. Just look around you; what brought them here? Tina, you can be damn sure they didn't come down here at dawn for my Po' Boys!" her New York accent flared.

As if on cue, a flock of hungry wharf gulls discovered the free donuts, chaotically dive-bombing the cadre of officials and developers feeding at the firepit. Over the din, Hugo could hear Carmen's laugh as he pushed on the nightclub doors. He knew her laugh well; it was more of an upwelling coming from deep inside. It had been a long time since he heard that laugh and he had wondered if he would ever hear it again.

6

Carefully placing the Borsalino on the gnarled mahogany bar top, Hugo straddled a stool at the counter. Toni had indeed remembered the sausages. Blinded by the glare of the morning light bleeding through the wall of old warehouse windows, a radiant apparition appeared at the far end of the bar, or was he real?

It took a minute for Hugo to recognize the lone patron. Seated no more than ten feet away was a real live urban legend eating breakfast, digging through a messy plate of over-easy while dipping his sourdough into a bowl of salsa, with a pint at the ready.

Awestruck, Hugo played it cool, looking straight ahead through the warehouse panes that illuminated the liquor bottles. They had a magnificent view of the new kid on the waterfront rising defiantly above McCovey Cove—San Francisco's latest phoenix, Pac Bell Park, home of the San Francisco Giants.

"It's a beautiful ballpark," said the old man. "The boys did well this year. They didn't win the pennant but damn if they didn't come close," He held up his pint glass in a toast.

"You got that right." Hugo saluted the ballpark with his coffee mug.

"I've heard of you," voiced the living legend. "You're 'the watchdog' the girls here talk about all the time." The old man pushed his crust through the river of yolk like a kid drawing on the sidewalk. "The Port wants Antonia and Teri out; been trying for years. Classic case of jurisdiction. Hell, you know all this. Hell, it's happened before," the legend's voice dropped. "It's the same old story."

Hugo got to his feet and stepped over to the old man, hand extended. "I've heard of you, too, sir. You worked for William Randolph Hearst. Hugo Sandoval."

"Call me Alfred, Al. Pleasure to meet you, Inspector."

The voice had been roughed up a bit by age, but Alfred Kleinen's grip was solid. "I was only a kid covering the streets in those days. Hearst took to a piece I wrote about the waterfront. The editor called me into the office on my day off. Hearst was on the line from Beverly Hills. Wanted to know if I'd made up the story."

"Did you?" Hugo was fascinated. For some reason he didn't think it out of line to question the ethics of a famous journalist.

"High and inside. You *are* direct," the old man chuckled. "Don't get me wrong, son, it's a good thing. It's part of your reputation." Kleinen pushed his plate away. "I'll tell you the story, Inspector, but how about a trade? Are you going to shut the girls down?" Toni appeared as if on cue, with fresh coffee.

Hugo was caught off guard. "Damn good coffee," he said as she filled both their mugs. He wanted to confide in this San Francisco icon, reveal what he had seen under the pier. But he needed Otis Street to put things in motion first.

"I'm working on it. I'll have to get back to you on that."

"Fair enough," said Kleinen. He slid the basket of sourdough and salsa to Hugo.

The meeting by the firepit had broken up. A few members of the tribunal cut through the bar to warm up before heading to their cars; Carmen was among them. She eyed Hugo's unfinished breakfast.

"No rush." Before leaving, she shot off an apologetic smile to the old man and in her best British accent, "I do hope I didn't interrupt."

"Not at all, my dear," Kleinen chuckled. "We're just trading stories. You're welcome to join us." Hugo stiffened involuntarily. Carmen must have sensed it.

"Lovely, but next time, I'm afraid. I'll leave you to it." Carmen turned to catch up with Josh Weston, the developer's architect who was holding the club's front door for her.

Hugo loved a good sourdough, and this one was excellent. He also loved the jazz piped into the bar. Classic bebop, *that's Dexter Gordon on sax,* he thought. But most of all he loved stories about his City; he collected them like some people collect stamps.

"What did you mean when you said, 'It's happened before?'" Hugo asked.

The newspaperman scratched his ear and began. "I couldn't have been more than twenty at the time, and newly married. It was late at night. I had been rounding the bars in the Barbary, having a few with the other blackmen."

"*Black* men?"

"It was what we called ourselves at the time. Our crew ran the presses over at the *Examiner* building throughout the night; got as much ink on us as on the paper. We looked like coal miners. It was hard work, but I needed the extra work. I only had a few stories a week printed at that time, and a new baby at home to feed."

Kleinen took a long pull on his beer to help him remember. "It was one of those nights where the fog paints you right to the pavement. You know those nights; I know you do. Steel streetcar wheels squealing against the tracks up Market Street, raspy voices of taxi horns and faint sirens; streetlights on the bridge strung like of dull pearls bleeding through the mist—and the smell. If I told you I loved the smell, I think you would understand. I'll never come clean of it," the old man said with a touch of melancholy. "A mixture of old mudflats and dreams."

Hugo remained silent.

"Well, walking home that night I hugged the waterfront," he went on, staring through the windowpanes. "The piers were calm, even peaceful; it was as if they were floating on glass. 'Between the tides' as they say. A few piers down, I sat on a piling under a streetlamp. I watched its golden light ripple all the way to Oakland. It was when I lit my cigarette that I saw him."

Hugo was in it now. He barely took a breath while the barkeep poured Al a fresh beer.

"It was the body of a man, face-down in the water. I tried to get a hold of him, but I needed help. No one was around so I hiked over the hill to Central Station. The police sergeant drove me back. He wanted to know everything, where I had been drinking and who I was with and what did I *think* I saw. When we got to the pier, the poor bastard was floating like a cork, right where I left him. We had a time getting him out of the water. Thank god he was a little guy, an old man, like me," Al laughed. "Chinese, dressed in kitchen whites; poor soul." With that, he toasted to the memory with his new pint, cutting his story short.

"You mentioned a jurisdiction problem," Hugo prompted, not wanting Al to end it there.

"I did indeed," Al laughed before darkening his tone. "The sergeant searched the cook's pockets and came up empty. No wallet, no ID, nothing. He turned him over a couple of times to see if he had been shot or stabbed or hit in some way. Again, nothing. I can tell you, Inspector, it made me damned uneasy. To top it off, the cop was rather rough about it. He didn't know I was a reporter or at least trying to be one, and he certainly didn't try to hide his prejudice. Absolutely no respect or compassion. When he called it in on his radio, the cursing and slurs were chilling. Hell, I just wanted to go home. I had never seen a dead body before and I was pretty shaken up by it—that, and the fog had started to settle into my bones. But I knew there was a story right in front of me and it was far from over."

Just then, the second owner of the bar slipped into the pit and pulled another beer from the tap, not for Hugo or the old man but for herself. A few years younger than her business partner, Teri was a stark contrast to the Sicilian—tall, blonde, lanky, but equally animated.

"I waited," Al continued. "Two more squad cars showed up, one with the captain. I couldn't hear their conversation until the captain pointed to me, "He's the one who found him? Then he's just the man to push him back in." Al stopped his story to take a sip. "And so I did," he added in a painful tone.

Teri, the tall, lanky barkeep, jumped in. "Al, you tellin' the Chief about the dead guy you found floating off Pier 15? It just hit me, that is exactly what we should've done this morning—pushed them all back in—all but this one," and winked at Hugo as she left the bar. She was wearing bike shorts like her partner.

"I better cut to the chase before the girls come back," said Al. "It had to be about four in the morning when the Coast Guard cutter showed up. They used a hook to pull the dead guy back out again; looked like they had done it plenty of times before. When the Coasties placed the body on the pier all hell broke loose. The police captain started strutting up and down the pier like he was marking his territory, barking to the Ensign on the boat, 'You can't put him on *my* pier; you pulled him out, it's your fish. You take him away!' his words."

Hugo cringed at the racist implications of the gaffe.

"I figured the police captain didn't want me to stick around to say I pushed him back *in* so I hightailed it out of there. Besides, the sun was near up and there was an outside chance I could slip into my flat without the wife waking up; if not, there would be hell to pay. I knew she would never believe a word of it, and I was right, she never did."

Outside, Carmen's shiny new Prius was dwarfed by the 1965 salmon-pink Lincoln Continental parked one over on Pier 50. The Lincoln looked like it was going through a ritual shedding of its fake leather roof, a snake peeling off its skin. Its faded yellow and black California plates cried, *original owner*. Hugo figured it belonged to his new acquaintance Alfred Kleinen. Judging by the dents and scrapes on the auto's body, he hoped Al lived nearby.

Hugo was pleased to see a bike rack mounted on the tail of

the Prius; his Gitane felt right at home. He knew his ex-wife loved bike riding almost as much as he did but her real hobby was her Bluetooth. Hugo could never tell if she were speaking to him or someone in Switzerland. As they pulled away from the Two Bits Bar & Cafe, he began to retell the old man's story, until he realized she was listening to her office assistant in her ear.

"I'm driving the inspector to Otis Street. Call me later, will you?" she said, apologetically pointing at her earpiece. He wondered when that would be.

As they approached the Lefty O'Doul Bridge a sudden flash of bells and lights signaled that the deck of the bridge was on the rise. A lone sailboat was making its way by motor down Mission Creek to the Bay.

"Yes, *that* inspector," she continued. "Brilliant. Uh huh. Yep. I'll be in the office in fifteen," she said before seeing the lowering arm of the bridge gate. "Maybe twenty. Yes, darling, please call me back then." Although Carmen casually used *darling* in her conversations, Hugo's ears perked up.

The Prius was the first and only car stopped by the barricade. Their front-row seats showcased the impressive Giants ballpark on the far shore of the creek flanked by the new housing projects Hugo questioned as "affordable," a buzzword he felt was often misused by developers to soothe public opinion.

Pulling the device from her ear, Carmen turned to her passenger, eyes dancing. "Thanks to your sideshow this morning, I'll be looking at emails the rest of the day on this." Her swimming-pool blue eyes drove him nuts and she knew it. He quickly looked away, pretending to examine the underbelly of the drawbridge. "Good lord, Hugo, you're not still phobic about bridges, are you?"

The man in the passenger seat was indeed uncomfortable but it wasn't the bridge itself or its height above the water that unnerved him; It was seeing Carmen again that threw him. *Fourteen months.* Hugo shifted in his seat and replied, "No. It's just—no."

"Interesting morning. You showed no hesitation jumping into that boat this morning. Honestly, Hugo, I am impressed. Now tell me about the old man you were sitting at the bar with, who is he?"

"You might say he's a bit of a cross between Horton and Hunter S. Thompson. It's a long story; I'll tell you later."

"A writer then? Brilliant. He did remind me of Hemingway when I first saw him."

"You know these women, the owners of the bar?" Hugo asked, "What's with the bike shorts?"

Carmen laughed. "They're cyclists, of course—like you, except they dress for it. Antonia and Teri met while riding. Remarkable they keep at it, considering,"

"Considering what?"

"You are joking," Carmen looked at Hugo. "You really don't know?" She leaned back in her seat to savor the moment. "Oh, my god, I know a story about this town you don't. How is it you never heard about this?"

"Let's have it."

"Ten years ago, the younger one—"

"Antonia."

"No, not the Italian, the tall one."

"Teri."

"Right Teri. About six, eight years ago, Teri is riding home after work but she's in a hurry and attempts to jump the creek when the bridge is on the rise. Almost makes it but she and her bike are too low and land in the armature below the deck on the other side. A homeless fellow who had been camped under the catwalk rescued her. Saved her life."

"You're telling me that fifty-something woman tried to jump this bridge—on a *bicycle*?"

"What's fifty got to do with it?" Carmen shot back. "Hugo, she broke everything in her body and lived to pour your coffee this morning."

"That's crazy." Hugo was impressed.

"No crazier than two independent women operating a barely solvent bar on prime waterfront land. I think they're cool, I do, but they are no match for my client or any other developer lusting after this pier. Sure, they've got a case against the Port for plumbing violations, but honestly, how far will that take them?

"What's your next move?" Hugo adjusted the Borsalino while the drawbridge settled into place.

"You mean my *client's* next move," she clarified.

"Yes, Water Rock Partners."

"It's not up to Water Rock. I'm not even sure we have the inside lane but whoever does can afford to be patient. Pier 50's waste lines spilling into the Bay brought the State and City to the table, brilliant, but Hugo, was it wise to publicly challenge the City on camera just to stall the eviction of a single tenant? The Port has made promises to Water Rock in good faith. It's only a matter of time, whether you red-tag Two Bits or not," said Carmen in her legal voice. "Inspector, the question is not what my client is going to do, but what *you* are going to do."

"Like I said before, it's up to the mayor."

The hum of the tires on the steel deck of the drawbridge was oddly comforting and allowed him to think about what Alfred Kleinen had said.

"Oh, tosh, no one alive knows more about the waterfront than you, or for that matter cares half as much," Carmen scoffed. "Besides, who else is she going to listen to? Certainly not that airhead Winslow." Carmen sounded annoyed. "And please tell me, what does that woman do at City Hall besides get paid? Honestly, Hugo. I have absolutely no idea."

"*Jurisdiction,*" Hugo muttered under his breath, his mind drifting as he watched the lone sailboat clear the waterway and enter the Bay.

"What's that, darling?" Carmen glanced over at her ex-husband a bit too long. While others were drawn to his handsome features, for Carmen it had always been the softness in his eyes that pulled her in.

Ping.

Hugo tilted the screen away from Carmen's curious eyes and let an awkwardness settle between them. It was a text from his own right hand, Sara at Otis Street.

News about Ava from T. Ray. B here soon?

Despite his concern for Ava, he hesitated to involve Carmen, yet this was his chance to prove he could put his family first. The couple finished the ride in Prius mode, running silent as they crossed the City to Hugo's office.

Carmen parked halfway down the no-name alley and waited for Hugo to unleash his Gitane. "Have you heard from Ava lately?" she asked casually as Hugo leaned on the driver's side window to say goodbye.

"No," Hugo lied. "You?"

"Not lately," replied Carmen, deliberately looking away.

Was she lying? Hugo couldn't tell. "Um. Thanks for the ride," Hugo said over his shoulder.

Although she knew it would be useless, she shouted after him, "Hugo Sandoval—get back here! What did you find under the pier?"

Fighting the street noise of Hugo's City, Carmen's voice was barely audible. By the time he turned around for one last look, she had ducked her head inside the hybrid like a turtle into its shell before silently swimming into the flow of traffic.

Switzerland.

7

FORT BRAGG HAD BEEN A SLEEPY TOWN since the lumbermill closed; perhaps a little too sleepy, thought T. Ray. Vacancies appeared to be the big new thing in this quaint coastal village. Empty storefronts were so common that he passed more buildings with For Lease signs than business shingles before arriving at the broken stone steps of The Joe, the town cafe. He texted Hugo before going inside,

you on the road yet?

T. Ray had been leading what his in-laws often described as a "retired life" in the wilds of Mendocino for thirty-odd years, but Hugo knew better. As a hybrid of private eye and forensic building contractor, T. Ray was unique. His instincts and investigative skills proved invaluable to Hugo's more troubled cases in the City. The pair had met as young men in the National Guard in the late 1970s when disasters and domestic disturbances were the business of their home state militia, not foreign wars. When Hugo's mentor sent him to the engineering department at San Francisco's City College, T. Ray pursued a less-institutional path to fit his tie-dyed, Buddha-meets-Thoreau search for reality. Despite his dubious reputation as a self-taught architect and artisan builder, it was T. Ray's boundless curiosity that colored his career.

The investigator was never more curious than on that crisp October morning. He wanted the full story on the whale before Hugo arrived and figured The Joe was as good a place to start as any. The café was packed with characters led by its owner Bella, who was a sponge for local gossip. He listened as the barista's strong mellifluous voice permeated the din in the popular joint with her running account of orders.

"Large soy latte for Derek! Bruno, come get your Americano, it's getting cold!"

T. Ray found the salty bleached blonde alluring in a *stranded on a desert island* sort of way, but he had far too much respect for Bella's leadership in the town to let his mind wander. And, of course, there was Daisy to consider. Yes, Daisy, the love of his life, twenty years and counting.

Reading people was a big part of his job. With stocking caps back in fashion, T. Ray had learned to decipher if the wearer was a fisherman or a "grower" by the cock of his sock. The long tail of a woven cap flopping down the neck was a sure sign of a pot grower, but today he was on the lookout for fishermen, and that meant caps fitted close to the head. It was good cap-fishing that morning; he caught at least four, maybe five in the cafe.

"Mr. Harrison, your macchiato is ready, dear—"

T. Ray drifted towards the forty-year-old in a tightly-rolled knit cap customer leaning on the counter. From his exposed features, as best T. Ray could tell, the man was a redhead. The burn on his cheeks, singed ear lobes and wraps on his hands told the investigator he was most likely a mate who worked the decks.

Bella worked the coffee bean dispenser in rhythm to the music. *Clack, clack, clack.*

Nearly breaking the rhythm, a young mother in hand-woven clothes with a baby swaddled somewhere inside them vied for Bella's attention. Once Bella was in the zone, the barista's octopus-like arms never stopped for the pour, drip, steam and pull.

"Could you remake this?" asked the mother. "I really need to go non-fat."

"No problem, I'll put it in the de-fatter." Bella laughed without missing a beat, catching T. Ray's twinkling eye at the bar.

"Captain Dave, your cappuccino. Cuban for Loretta. Bruno!"

"What's the news from the coast on the stranding?" T. Ray asked Bella hoping others would hear and join in.

"Loretta just told me it's a *blue* just below Ten Mile. Ninety feet long if it's an inch," replied Bella, steaming milk. "As soon as I close, I'm heading out for a look."

The bearded, stocking cap guy at the window table chimed in sagaciously. "Ah, the sea will find her and take her out soon enough. Nature takes care of its own, Bella."

"I'm not so sure, Dave. I hear she's wedged in there *pre-tt-ee* tight. Besides, we've got the low tides for the next two weeks, so how the hell is the sea to reach her?" Loretta perched, elbows on the counter on the lee side of T. Ray, her forearms covered in tattoos.

"She? You saw the whale?" asked T. Ray.

"Nah, Crystal called me; told me the blue got stuck in Chicken Cove. She runs her dogs every morning along those bluffs. My place is north of Ten Mile. It's a bit of a hike from the road and it's almost impossible to get down to the beach, too hard on this old girl," Loretta said as she shifted to her good leg. "Besides, that's the Dillon Ranch and they are particular about who comes on their land uninvited—especially strangers. All I can say is that blue couldn't have picked a rougher more inhospitable part of the coast."

"Hey, Bel, Bruno remembered he had to pick up his kids at school; minimum day or something," Old Ben said. "Put another shot in his and I'll drink it." For nearly a decade Old Ben had claimed his own territory at the far end of the counter, a choice spot with a wall to lean on, and the only barstool with a back.

"You know if this heat keeps up, she could blow," offered Captain Dave, adding, "I say we help her along, problem solved." Dave was known as not the most optimistic of fishermen. Some would say his comment reflected his weak catch year after year while others would suggest that Dave's gruesome conclusion suited his dour temperament.

"Yeah, unless you're one of the new vacation rentals, or that new winery downwind— 'cuz if she blows, she's going to stink to high heaven!" charged Loretta. "It's not good for business; keeps the tourists away. We're barely out of a recession; we need a plan!"

"Three or four sharks could easily polish off that carcass and not have to feed for another year," piped in Old Ben, who had left his doughnut too long in the cup and was forced to retrieve it with a spoon.

"You've been watching the Discovery Channel again, Ben? Here's a thought, maybe Cate's grandson can turn the carcass into an art project," said Bella with a wink to T. Ray.

"What's that, Bel?" asked T. Ray, puzzled.

Bella nodded to The Joe's "Wall of Fame," mostly a gallery of fading snapshots of smiling fishermen holding up their catch and Little Leaguers posing with trophies. But in the middle was a framed clipping from the *Fort Bragg Advocate Journal.* The headline read, "Beach Artist Slides Home Safe." T. Ray walked over to the wall for a closer look at the photo of a man climbing out a cockeyed kitchen window and landing headfirst on a beach, half-dressed. The caption identified the man as local resident Nate Dillon. *That name again*, T. Ray noted.

The chatter went on for another shot or two but no one at The Joe had heard anything about a marine biologist or her Airstream parked at Chicken Cove.

"If your scientist friend is out there, she might have more to contend with than a stranded whale, if you catch my drift," said Bella.

He didn't.

"I don't see her in town much anymore, but I know for a fact

Cate Dillon still rules her part of the coast," Bella added before resuming her morning routine.

As the son of a son of a North Coast lumberman, T. Ray knew to take the barista's warning seriously. With a nod to Bella and to Jimmy Buffett's *Sailor* song in his head, T. Ray tossed a twenty on the counter and left the raucous comfort of The Joe for the Dillon ranch.

8

ON THE AFTERNOON BEFORE THE MIDDLE OF THE NIGHT barrage of calls and texts to her father, Ava had parked her Airstream on the headlands of the historic Dillon Ranch just a few strides from the precarious cliff, which towered thirty feet above Chicken Cove. Earlier that same morning, the North Coast Marine Institute had officially put Ava in charge of the whale-stranding event. It had taken the fledgling marine biologist most of the day to outfit her trailer, coordinate her team and gain the critical clearances from the NOAA Fisheries Regional Office before she could embark on her adventure to the remote cove.

It had been a long day for Ava since the dawn alert of the stranded leviathan. An adrenaline rush propelled her physically for the first twelve hours, but, as it wore off, she had trouble reining in her emotions. Her first tears of the day flowed before she even left the institute with the ship-to-shore call from the captain of the NOAA vessel, when he confessed his ship hit the blue whale. She could hear the captain fighting tears of his own when he confirmed the strike wound from his ship's hull was near its head.

It wasn't until late in that first day that Dr. Ava Rose Sandoval and her herding dog Lobo arrived at the gate to the Dillon Ranch.

She could finally relax after the two-hour ordeal of towing her twenty-three-foot Flying Cloud north along the serpentine Pacific Coast Highway to the cove where the 50-ton dead blue whale waited patiently. The Flying Cloud had been a gift from her parents after receiving her PhD at Monterey Bay's Hopkins Marine Station. When she left for the field station of the North Coast Marine Institute, the Airstream had become her sanctuary on wheels—laboratory, library, communications center—and home.

Just six weeks before the stranding at Chicken Cove, Ava had been assigned a visiting artist at the institute. Her job was to advise as to where he could install his sculptures on the campus. The artist turned out to be Nate Dillon, a sculptor recently returned from Ireland to his home on the North Coast. A few beach walks and campfires later, the two had barely adjusted to each other when the blue whale threw them into the deep end of their new romance.

With sundown nearing, Ava steered her truck and Flying Cloud through the ranch gate. She waved at Nate who was feeding a few head of cattle off the back of his truck. He took off his wide-brimmed ranch hat and waved back, *just like in the movies*, she thought. Besides the cattle Nate was feeding, Ava counted six or seven sheep on the headlands, their heads intent on the patchy coastal prairie. A small flock for a ranch that size but big enough for a herding dog. When she set Lobo free, the pup ran like the wind, running in circles around the startled sheep. Ava laughed at her dog's joy and further restored her own weary body with the sea air rising from the deep cut in the coastline that could only be Chicken Cove.

Watching her lover run across the crusty dry grassland to greet her, Ava thought he looked terribly lean and boyish, a modern-day Gary Cooper with a little Sam Shepard mixed in. Not to appear too eager, she welcomed his kiss while he leaned on her rig.

"If there's still light, we'll go down to the beach to see her but let's get you settled first," Nate said, beaming and telling her how he had spent the morning leveling a flat, solid pad for her Airstream and had scraped a nearby area for the fleet of whale watchers that would most surely follow.

With *Dillon Brothers Dairy* scrolled in faded script on its doors, the old ranch flatbed led the caravan to the designated parking spot near the cliff. As Ava followed slowly across the rocky pasture, she became curious about the strange sticks and mossy branches lying on top of the last of the hay in the dairy truck's bed.

Once the trailer was stabilized, she handed Nate a beer from the Flying Cloud's original icebox. "Who have I been dating, cowboy or artist?"

He laughed. "It helps to be both, I think. Collecting keeps the balance. The forests and the beaches are rich with natural art on their own. I just gather the spoils," he said modestly.

"You do far more than that; I've seen your sculptures, remember?" Then she came to the point. "Nate, what can you tell me about that red tag on the seat of your truck? None of my business, of course, but it caught my eye. Did you know my dad wanted me to be a building inspector?"

"Funny, I'm not quite sure what my dad wanted me to be," Nate replied.

"Tell me about your dad, then. I don't know a thing about him—or about this beautiful ranch. Will you at least tell me that?"

"Well, how much do you already know?"

"Only what's on Wikipedia," Ava laughed. "It said your family had operated the largest dairy on the North Coast in its day, running a thousand head of sheep and cows. That was about it."

"The ranch has been in the family since the Depression. Gran is the only one left."

"I don't see a thousand head of sheep," Ava said. "Just a handful now. What happened?"

Nate didn't answer.

When Ava tucked in close to the cowboy, there was a sweet awkwardness between them. It eased with their laughter when

Lobo raced between them, chasing a covey of quail with his clumsy enthusiasm.

"It's getting late," Nate said to change the subject.

"You said your gran was the only one left. Where do *you* fit into all this?" she looked up at his soft brown eyes. She loved the faint freckles on his cheekbones; at a distance, they looked like shadows.

"I'm just the end of a long story," said Nate, again evading the question. Ava tapped the passenger side of the truck where the word *Dairy* had faded into the worn body of the green truck.

She had won. Nate opened up.

"Two brothers from Ireland settled here about 100 years ago. It was only a patchwork of coastal prairie and redwood forest back then. The younger of the brothers was my grandfather, Jacob Delany Dillon. J.D. for short. My dad told me that J.D. and his older brother Sean worked as cutters for a lumber baron for seven years to pay off the ranch. It was dangerous work, but they were still young men when they ended up with the seven hundred acres we're standing on—and they were no older than I am now."

"And a farmhouse, the one across the highway?"

"The farmhouse was already here of course, built in the 1880s along with the big horse barn. A few other outbuildings go back even further. The ranch covers the headlands and a good bit of land up there in the hills. It was a dream location, only ten miles south to town and another mile to the harbor. Back then, Fort Bragg was a lumber company town; still is, for the most part but times change. Gran always says it was a good life, but hard."

"Your family found a sweet spot, no doubt about it," said Ava looking out to the shimmering sea.

Nate smiled at her innocence.

"For a thousand years, the Yuki ritually burned and weeded the grasses. When my folks arrived, it was ideal pastureland for the dairy stock they planned to ship here from Ireland. Add to that, all the lumber they needed for new barns and outbuildings could be cut in the hills; they were set. It was the perfect ranch; now it can barely support a small herd of sheep." Nate kicked the dry crust of the land with his boot.

Ava wanted to put a spin on his frustration. "You were born here on the ranch. It's a part of you."

Nate nodded to the Victorian across the road. "I was born in the big house. I must have been going on four when Dad built the cottage out near the cliff," he nodded toward the stand of trees near Chicken Point. "The three of us lived in the cottage until my mother died."

"How old were you?"

"Ten," he smiled thinking of his mother. "When I was a kid, she would send me out to check on the sheep. My favorite thing was to hunt for arrowheads. Sometimes I came across a snare, or a rock used for a tool; they were scattered all over the land."

"That explains a lot," said Ava, thinking of Nate's sculptures.

He smiled shyly, "I guess so." Seeing Ava had drifted, he stopped his story there.

While the beach artist climbed on the roof of the Airstream to secure the satellite dish, Ava locked Lobo in the trailer before walking to the cliff's edge. The young marine biologist was thinking that the name of the cove was a perfect fit.

"And did young Nate ever play 'chicken?'" she asked when Nate joined her.

She could see that the outcrop of rocks at the entrance to Chicken Cove created a death-defying approach from the open sea. Even the most agile of marine mammals would find it difficult, if not impossible to reach the safety of the cove. But there she was, the blue whale's body resting peacefully on the tidepools.

"Sweet darlin', how did you manage it?" Ava whispered to the precious creature below, wiping her eyes, fighting both fatigue and the sea breeze.

After seeing the whale from the cliff, Ava had more questions for the ship's crew. Their captain had told her two of his deckhands had witnessed the whale surface after the hit and told him *she* was still alive although struggling to go deep. It was time for Ava to take a closer look.

Nate could not help but be impressed as he watched Ava fearlessly descend the steep cliff to the tidepool. It had been a lonely life for the young salvage artist but here was a woman who challenged his loneliness.

Nate scoured the pools with an eye for sculpture materials. Holding his camera high above his head, he slowly walked towards Ava and her whale, never mind that the Pacific was a biting fifty-four degrees. The artist barely flinched; the images captured by his lens were too inviting. His camera caught the whale's tail half out of the water, then the cetacean's head resting on the sand, now onto Ava. Nate captured her just as she ran her hands over the wound. He caught her just as she rested her own head on the head of the leviathan but when Ava climbed onto the whale's back, Nate stopped shooting.

"Ava, get down from there! She's rolling!" The very next wave rocked the whale and sent Ava flying into the tidepools.

"Whoa! Ava, are you okay?" He helped her to the narrow stretch of beach.

"Golly, that was stupid," Ava laughed nervously. "Nate, we need to stabilize her if we're going to keep her."

"*Keep her?* Please tell me you're joking!"

But she wasn't.

When they reached the top of the cliff, they looked down on the scarred and mottled blue whale. "Oh, my," Ava sighed. Soaked and shivering, the scientist was seized with sorrow.

As he put a truck blanket around her shoulders, "It's up to the house with you. A hot shower then I'll show you the town," Nate vigorously rubbed her wet back. "Trust me, after warm brandy down at the pub, you'll be fine," letting the Irish in him surface.

"Not tonight. Don't worry, I'm good here," Ava said gratefully to Nate, the only other creature of any size within reach, a more lumbering two-legged type than the blue whale but equally as shy. Wiping her nose, she tried to hold back, but the tears came anyway. As Nate hugged her, her whole body sighed in his arms. He kissed her gently on her forehead.

Quickly recovering her balance, she asked again, "Nate, when are you going to tell me about that red tag on the seat of your truck? It's your cottage, your art studio, right? You should let me help."

"It's nothing, Ava. Get some rest. I need to stay at the big house with Gran tonight but call me on the landline if you need me for anything. All right? And hey, keep Lobo with you, don't let him wander." He didn't know Ava well, but he knew enough to know that her stubborn streak was strong. "Don't test these cliffs. In fact, both of you stay clear of the cove. I'll be back in the morning," he warned. And with a quick kiss, he left her.

Ava sensed an ominous underpinning to the young rancher's words. After all, Nate knew very well she had lived alone on the coast for nearly two years, more than enough time to respect the instability of California's untamed cliffs—so why had he changed his tone and what was he hiding behind the red tag?

Heedless of Nate's warning, a worried Ava struck out on the cliff's footpath with Lobo at her side. She had hoped the rich mix of sea and land would restore her thinking before calling her father. It was a tough call to make after months of silence, but Ava was feeling the pressure from the institute and now from Nate. Even the position of the whale inside the tidepools itself bothered her. Ava needed her curious dad to show up along with his alter ego, the celebrated building inspector. By morning, the three of them might be able to sort out whatever this was she had walked into.

9

CARMEN HAD DROPPED OFF HUGO in the alley on the backside of the otherwise resplendent Department of Building Inspections, known by those who would dare file for a building permit in the City as *the fucking DBI.* Containing 278 employees, the DBI had recreated itself with a new headquarters and a new name in a thinly veiled attempt to distance the revived agency from years of corruption and controversy. Despite its slick modern façade and expensive technology-infused infrastructure, the sorely needed restoration of faith in the City's building department was to be found anchored in a remote corner on the fifth floor.

Hugo leashed his Gitane to an electrical service pipe next to a dingy metal door fronting on the alley named Otis Street. Out of public view, he punched a code into a lock below the ominous and sacrosanct EMERGENCY EXIT ONLY stencil. Five flights up the hollow stairwell, a winded Hugo reached his sanctum. As per department policy, numbered doors on each landing remained locked—all but Floor 5, which, on that morning, was cracked open by an autographed copy of *The Wild Parrots of Telegraph Hill,* hardbound edition; signed.

Once inside the office his assistant, the calm and evocative Sara Dunne, greeted him. Sara's petite stature and multiple tattoos were deceiving. Known as Hugo's right hand, his "No. 1" for years, Sara ceremoniously disarmed both delivery boys and elected officials with a smile, but by the end of their visits they all knew who was running Otis Street and left the offices feeling grateful she had tolerated their intrusion.

"The red tag order for Two Bits Bar & Cafe is on your desk ready to go," Sara leaned on the mahogany and chip-glass framework which separated her office from Hugo's while he scrolled through a morning flurry of emails on his laptop.

"Um. Any calls?"

"Almost all Pier 50 this morning, Chief." She rolled her shoulders to relieve the tension. "I reminded the mayor and the others that it is Friday and, as they are fully aware, you do *not* have office hours on Fridays."

"Exactly right, No. 1. I am *not* here. Who called?"

Sara read off the messages almost without further editorial. "Two guys named Jake, one from the Port and one from the Police Commissioner's office; both misused and overused the word, *gulls*." She paused before moving on. "And you got a call from the environmental attorney for the new Pier 50 development," she said casually.

"Carmen. Right. When did that come in?"

"Less than a minute before you walked in the door." Sara paused to gauge his reaction. "She said she would call you back later." He was inscrutable, which was infuriating, but she let it go.

"Moving on, or rather backwards, Her Honorable the Mayor called about a half hour ago; she said you would know what it was about. Right on the mayor's designer heels, Celia Winslow, with two calls. The second call was to tell me her first call was private," Sara's tone reflected her dislike of Celia. Again, no reaction from her chief.

"Ahh, and Mrs. Tiao called. She insisted that the circular brick-work in the intersection of Judah and 37th Avenue is, and I quote, 'Yet another waste of taxpayer money. Tell the Chief, the aliens have already landed'."' Sara leaned back to enjoy that comment while Hugo took it in stride.

"I was just out in the Bay with her son." Hugo shook his head with a hint of a smile.

"She did mention that fact," Sara confirmed. Mrs. Tiao was one of Sara's favorites—one of a handful of callers who turned to Otis Street as if it were a combination confessional, complaint department, and information booth at the county fair. Sara took it all in stride, believing it was part of public service championed at Otis Street. "I transferred Mrs. Tiao to engineering. Chief, don't you think it odd, with her son being a fire captain, that she would complain about marking the underground water reserves?"

Hugo looked up at his trusty right hand, with his trademark circumspect smile. Sara took that as a yes.

"Next, Captain Tiao called to have me check on your tetanus status, which I did; you're good for another two years. Come clean, Chief," Sara came forward and sat on his desk. "What happened out there?"

"Under or on top of the pier?"

"Both, please." She had already taken note of the inspector's unusually untidy condition. After removing the wet-rimmed Borsalino, she noticed Hugo's hair shot out in all directions. He may not need a tetanus, but he was long overdue for a haircut. And were those egg stains on his crisp white shirt? Over-easy was her best guess.

Without taking his eyes away from hers, Hugo produced a small cobalt blue bottle from his pocket and carefully placed it on the desk. Sara reached for the bottle still caked with Bay silt; she was fascinated.

"That beauty is from *under* the pier; it was wedged into the seawall," Hugo said proudly then paused briefly before delivering the second bombshell. "On *top,* I had a fascinating conversation with Alfred Kleinen at the bar."

Sara gasped, "He's not just a legend, he's real—and still alive?" Hugo nodded to both. Astonished, Sara lost her composure. "Shut up! What did you talk about?"

Hugo had noticed in the past for whatever reason, Sara was always fired up on Fridays, but that morning he put her over the top.

"I think he was trying to help me in his own way; point me in a direction, if that makes any sense. I'll fill you in later," said the inspector in reflecting mode, while Sara studied the tiny blue vessel in the window light of Otis Street.

"Hello," said Sara in a hushed voice. "It looks like there is a glassmaker's mark on the bottom," she said, trying to mask her excitement. "Chief—?"

"Mmm. That might help date that section of the seawall; see what you can find out. Call the mayor; tell her I need a few days to research a new angle to Pier 50. Tell her—tell her I said she will be pleased," and with that, Hugo tucked the bottle and the unsigned red tag order for the Two Bits Bar + Café in his top drawer.

"Sara, who do we know on the Historic Preservation Commission?"

"I could call Reese."

"Good. Excellent. No. 1, dig in. Ask him to find out what constitutes a historic structure worthy of preservation."

"You mean, like a seawall?" Sara said, delighted.

"Clever girl! And see what Reese knows about Pier 50—and Sara, ask why it was excluded from the Port's Embarcadero Historic District."

"It's not in the HD?" she asked, surprised.

"Nope. Some idiot stopped at 48; I guess the creek threw 'em."

Sara retrieved a satchel from her office and dropped it on Hugo's well-ordered desk. On a Wednesday or a Thursday there would have been no room to do so without smashing precious documents. But on Fridays, the Chief agreed to work in the field. Sara used Fridays to clean up his desk, update the scrapbook wall, and, in general, organize all the open projects from the preceding week. Come Monday, her boss had the freedom to refill every surface to his heart's content with newspapers, maps, folders and the like throughout the week. It was a little ritual they shared. Although not quite noon, Sara had already restored order to Hugo's office sanctuary which now featured a worn leather satchel in the middle of his desk.

"Explain." Hugo stared at the satchel.

"There was one more phone message this morning, from Harrison, who told me that you are needed up north through the weekend." Sara watched the inspector's face change in response to T. Ray's call. "He was quite animated about it and suggested I put together your go-bag."

"I have a go-bag?" asked Hugo.

"You do now."

Hugo dug through the satchel filled with a fresh change of clothes, toiletries, cell phone charger, cash, maps and water, all that he would need for a few days outside city limits. When he finished inspecting the bag, Sara handed him the office first aid kit.

"You might need this again," indicating Hugo's bandaged hand.

"Good, you and Harrison saved me a trip back to the flat. Thank you, Sara."

"Chief, is Ava alright?" She could see that he was worried.

Hugo rounded the desk to take hold of the worn padded handles of his squeaky desk chair, but he didn't sit down.

"Yeah. Sure. I'm sure everything's fine. I just need to check on her. Don't worry. Call Bob: I need a car right away. Tell him I'll be there in ten. Is there anything else before I go?"

Sara flipped through her notebook "Rocco called."

"Hold on, crab season doesn't open for another month. What did he say?"

"He just said it was 'urgent.'" Sara made air quotes.

Rocco always said it was urgent. A close family friend, and Hugo's godfather, Rocco was a first-generation Italian who had cut his teeth with Hugo's old man on the docks. "I'll call him on my way out of town." Hugo took a deep breath.

"Keep your phone handy, will you, Sara? I have a feeling I'll be needing you this weekend," he said exiting the office the way he entered, go-bag firmly gripped by his good hand.

10

TEN MINUTES AFTER LEAVING OTIS STREET, Hugo walked under the deliriously happy circus flags flapping above Beautiful Bob's Used Car lot. Bob had fixed up the inspector with a one-year-old ash gray BMW he got on a sweet repo deal and was showing Hugo some ins and outs of the BMW, when he had to ask.

"Chief, when you going to evict that couple living in your Volvo? I'm happy to set you up with a loaner anytime, you know that, but when I walked by your car last week, they were tailgating. They had friends over, hot dogs grilled on a camp stove, the whole nine yards!" When the lighthearted Bob turned serious, his voice lowered, "Chief, they were playing scrabble on your hood! You are a good person, the best, but people take advantage of you. This couple, nice people for sure, but they need to get their own place before winter. Maybe I should help you with that."

Hugo laughed. "I'll think about it, Robo." Using Bob's nickname was a reminder that, like Hugo, Bob had grown up on the streets and to show a little more compassion for the family living in the Volvo. "And I appreciate the loaner; I owe you."

"You know it's the other way around. I'm just trying to look out for you, Chief. You know if you ever do move your car, you give me a heads-up, right? That is one helluva parking spot," laughed the dapper used car salesman.

Bob had chosen a bright blue shiny bow tie to match his Hawaiian shirt but Hugo felt something was askew. It took the normally observant inspector a minute before he realized Bob's version of Casual Friday came with a homespun tie pulled right off the lot's string of circus flags.

On that suspiciously calm morning in October, Hugo drove through the russet red towers of the Golden Gate with mixed feelings of love and loss as he watched his City dissolve in the rear-view mirror; *uncomfortable* feelings echoed by the aircraft carrier that passed 245 feet below the deck of the bridge. The flattop heading out to sea flanked by a fleet of ships, made Hugo wonder, *how could whales possibly get out the way of such an armada?*

11

THE BMW MADE THE DRIVE EFFORTLESS, almost seductive. Hugo had forgotten how calming a road trip could be. It was more than two hours before he reached the Pacific Coast Highway, where he followed the asphalt ribbon north along the magnificent Mendocino Coast. The more-than-capable Sara Dunne had mapped his route and taped it to the skin of an apple for the road. Navigation was simple, even for the reluctant adventurer, but Hugo appreciated the reassuring guide. And, most of all, the apple.

He was glad to be distracted by things other than Otis Street, Ava, and Carmen. Once clear of Bay Area traffic and the 101 corridor, the Wine Country opened to the determined BMW. He knew 2011 had been a rough year for wine grape growers and despite September's brief heat wave, heavy rains were in the forecast. From the freeway Hugo could see crews scrambling to harvest the grapes before the crop was ruined. Along the old frontage roads, vineyards surrounded the grand entrances to wineries further scored with impressive spires of undulating Italian cypress and out-of-place king palms.

Ping.

marine institute unable to confirm Ava's location; will keep you informed - #1

Cutting towards the coast, a parade of weathered barns led Hugo through the twists and turns of the deep redwoods along the Navarro River. As magnificent the ride through the redwood forest proved to be, the adventurous city kid in him was relieved to be in the open again at last, with the endless sea stretching to the horizon.

Thank god, was Hugo's gut response upon seeing the Pacific free from the shroud of the forest. It was the same feeling of relief he felt every time he left the tight canyons of the City's downtown core for the waterfront. A champion of a low to mid-rise urban habitat, Hugo had watched helplessly as tower after tower closed in the sky above the City. His only solace was his precious San Francisco waterfront had defiantly remained open and true to its historic roots; he vowed to keep it that way if he could.

Admittedly his driving was rusty from the years of relying on his bike or public transportation to get around the City. He could barely recall the last time he had taken an open road and here he was navigating the famous Coast road's demanding dips and skirting the perilous overlooks. But he didn't slow down. Even when passing the handful of weathered coastal villages or crossing creeks and rivers, he kept his foot on the gas without a thought as to how the drainage had been engineered. The anxious father focused on reaching the fishing harbor at the Noyo River and hearing news of his daughter.

The Noyo River Bridge that spanned its open mouth to the sea was reassuring in its solid but graceful arch. Its box girder construction tethered the bluffs on either side with its concrete arms stretching hundreds of feet above the water.

Below, at river's edge, Hugo found T. Ray waiting inside the Blue Crab Shack.

Although the blue of the Cape Cod exterior was for the tourists, the interior of the Blue Crab—from fir plank floor to pine rafters; red-checkered vinyl tablecloths to personal photos on the wall—was for the locals, along with the no-view bar in the back of the joint which sported a television. T. Ray had chosen a window table, which afforded a prime view of the bridge and the gooseneck of the river, with its parade of commercial fishing boats and private rigs. Hugo studied the traffic as a Coast Guard cutter and even a paddleboard joined in the run across the fresh and saltwater mix as it spilled into the Pacific.

"Doesn't look like it from here, but this harbor entrance is one of the most dangerous on the West Coast. The Coasties use it for training, period. See that jetty out there? I can tell you from personal experience it gets hammered."

The waitress brought plates. Hugo's order was the special combo—fish 'n' chips with calamari, a side of slaw and a cup of local chowder. Flanked by fisheries, the restaurant smelled of the catch; how could it not? To his surprise, Hugo found the clam chowder smooth and the calamari light and crispy.

"Harrison, we're *moving*," Hugo mentioned off-handedly to T. Ray who was nursing a mid-day hangover with his second Blue Crab remedy of a fried egg on burnt toast. Hugo would soon learn that the investigator had spent the better part of the afternoon fishing for information at the pubs in town before reaching his limit.

"It's just the incoming tide. We're on piers," reassured T. Ray. "Sandoval, this place remind you of Red's at all?" He could see Hugo was getting impatient.

"Okay, Harrison, let me have it. Did you find her? Is Ava okay?"

"She's fine," T. Ray hesitated. "But there are a few ins and outs. The whale for one, obviously, and then there's this red tag business."

"You're stalling, Harrison. Where did Ava park the Airstream exactly?"

"She parked it on a sheep ranch not fifteen minutes up the Coast from here."

"You're telling me they red-tagged a sheep ranch?"

T. Ray was evasive. "Not exactly. The ranch is over a thousand acres and runs a good stretch of the coastline. It so happens one of its structures is a cottage, which is where the rancher found the red tag yesterday.

"Okay. But what does that have to do with my daughter?"

"The cottage is on a point above the cove where the whale washed up. But wait, it gets better. Ava knows the rancher; in fact, he was the one who called her about the whale."

"Let's go, Harrison." Hugo started to push back his chair.

"Hang on. Before we go see your girl you need to meet someone," said T. Ray, gesturing toward the dark bar.

T. Ray walked over to speak with the bartender and shook hands with one of the men perched on a stool, a big fella. From where Hugo sat, it looked like T. Ray had bought him a round.

The waitress returned to refill their water glasses. When she did, Hugo noticed the small tattoo on the inside of her left wrist, *Gertrude*.

When she moved onto the next table, T. Ray asked Hugo, "Just how much do you know about the North Coast?"

"What's there to know?" Hugo tasted his first Scrimshaw; a Pilsner brewed a mile and a half north of the Blue Crab.

"After I located Ava, I checked into this whale business,"T. Ray said with hesitation. "It's complicated."

"Whales do wash up on beaches, don't they? How complicated could it be?"

"Well, let me put it this way. There was a whale washed up on a beach three, four years ago; not far from here. It was a fin whale, hit by a ship. Big son of a bitch, over sixty feet long,"T. Ray took a swig from Hugo's bottle. "He came ashore on a large open beach which is very unusual for this part of the coast. It's not Ocean Beach by any measure but it's a beach big enough and flat enough to drive on. Well, the North Coast being what it is, the fin's bad luck didn't end there."

"It got complicated," Hugo tried to move the story along.

"Exactly. That's when some yahoos showed up in their trucks and did just that."

"Did what?"

"Drove over the whale just for fun. The fin got pretty chewed up, from what I heard."

T. Ray could see his story angered Hugo.

"A retired schoolteacher was driving by the beach when one of the trucks pulled into the highway right in front of her. The yutz broke his rear wheel on the berm at the edge of the roadbed and subsequently flipped the whale's tail completely out of the truck bed and onto the highway. The old girl had to slam on her brakes; practically slid into it. She recognized the pair of jackasses as boys she taught in grade school and made them put the tail back on the beach."

Disturbed by the story, Hugo pushed away his unfinished calamari.

"That very night, the sea took the fin whale back home." T. Ray pulled Hugo's calamari within reach and doused it with Screaming Dave's #2, his go-to hot sauce from hell. Apparently, the hangover remedies had worked through his system.

Hugo looked at T. Ray, puzzled.

"There are lots of players in the game, Sandoval," said T. Ray. Before he could explain further, T. Ray's bar buddy joined them, beer in hand.

Hugo thought the man standing at their table a spitting image of the redwood burl sculpture stationed outside the door to the Blue Crab. He kept the observation to himself, noting the swagger in the big man's step.

"Skip, this is the fella I was telling you about. Inspector Hugo Sandoval."

The big man nodded, and they shook hands.

Henshaw, once seated, began without hesitation. "*Tango II* is my boat. Ya can't see her from here, she's parked upriver. Henshaws have been on the water for three generations now and with my boy Moses coming on, that makes four," he said proudly.

Hugo noticed Henshaw's grip hand, dampened with beer, had tattoos on his knuckles and a striking scar where the thumb had been reattached.

"As I told you earlier, Inspector Sandoval's daughter is the marine biologist who is going to figure out what to do with that whale up in Chicken Cove," said T. Ray. "Skip, tell him what you told me this morning,"

"Like I said, we was fishing off the rocks just north of Chicken Cove Thursday afternoon. I had the boy under in the kelp, bagging urchins. My job on deck is to keep his air line clear and hold position. Dangerous water there. Lots of crags near the edge of the sanctuary." The captain of the *Tango II* took a swig, foam catching the curls in his beard. "I know what you're thinking, fellas, but I've fished these waters my whole life and I know 'xactly where that boundary is but I gotta push it, you see. Got a family to feed so I went right to the edge."

Hugo thought he sounded more angry than defensive.

T. Ray prodded. "Tell the inspector about the ship."

"Right. The daylight was gone you see, but we was finally pulling up some numbers so me and my boy, we kept fishin'. I was checking the stern line when I looked up and saw lights from a ship off the cove. She was in close, inside the sanctuary, almost inside the cove. Good size, too, from what I could tell. Not many ships out here that big so I figured it was the research boat that has been hanging around. We seen it all over the water last couple months mapping the floor but if it was her, she weren't mapping, no way."

"How do you know that?" asked Hugo.

"Mapping is sonar, Inspector. Quiet on the water, on the top at least. That night I heard the ship's gears and they was screamin' for all to hear. Whoever she was, that boat was working her winches hard, pulling with all her might. Then nothing. The screeching stopped. Damn weird thing."

"Pulling what do you think?" Hugo found Henshaw fascinating.

"The whale, sir, the whale. Only thing it could have been. I didn't know it at the time of course, but like I said it was dark, and I had Moses under."

"Were any other boats out there besides you and this mystery ship?" Hugo asked.

"Hard to tell. Didn't see nobody. Anyway, the sea started kicking up her skirt and we had to go. Barely made it back in time before the storm."

Henshaw drained the bottle for emphasis. "One thing you gotta understand, you can't just pick up anchor and go poke your nose in someone else's business," he said, staring at Hugo. "Specially on the water."

"Anything else, Skip?" T. Ray poked a little more.

The crusty fisherman looked down the throat of his empty bottle. "Now that I think about it, by the time Moses was on deck, the ship was gone. I told him about it, but there was no ship for him to see. He probably thought at the time I was crazy. Rounded Chicken Point I figured, but what I do know is that ship headed south 'cuz nothing passed me that night."

"Skip, why would a research boat, or any boat, for that matter, attempt to tow a whale out to sea?" Hugo's mind was starting to make connections.

"That's the question, ain't it? Bothered me all night. I checked in with the Coast Guard when we got to harbor. They told me the NOAA research boat reported hitting a whale Wednesday, midday, so I was right. Damn shame. Come daylight I sent my boy down to have a good look into the cove from the cliff. Sure enough, Moses told me she lay on the beach in Chicken Cove, said he could see where the *gaffs* were placed near the tail to hook her up." Skip's mug was drained but it looked like T. Ray was done buying.

"She?" Hugo asked as the captain of *The Tango II* got up to go.

"Yeah, 'she.' My boy told me her calf was stretched out alongside her. Fifteen feet if she were an inch. He said the calf was pure white like an albino and tucked into her mother like we seen 'em out on the water."

Hugo looked at T. Ray, who just raised his eyebrows and said nothing. After the big man was out of range, T. Ray whispered to Hugo, "Let's go catch up with your girl. This I got to see."

It was a good thing that T. Ray was driving, Hugo thought. Although the entrance to the sandy, overgrown roadbed was exactly as Ava described in her text that afternoon, he would have certainly missed the turn.

turn west 4.5 miles north of the Blue Crab on the PCH, between the Monterey cypress stump and the lichen-covered boulder

T. Ray gave Hugo some local history along the way. "Until a few months ago, Jack Dillon ran the ranch, or what was left of it. The dairy used to operate in those big barns back in the day, but it hasn't been in business since '89 when Jack's father passed. The creeks run most seasons, water enough for their livestock, but what I heard was that Jack couldn't keep the animals fed the past few years. I'm still tracking that down, along with a few other rumors."

T. Ray didn't like to speculate, but he needed to fill Hugo in on local gossip, "Jack Dillon was killed in a car crash up the coast earlier this year. The sheriff's report labels the accident as suspicious. Most everyone I ran across agrees."

"Alcohol?" asked Hugo.

"I don't think so. I heard from a couple of folks in town that Jack had been sober for years."

"Family?"

T. Ray pointed to the pitched roofs of the historic ranch peering out from a magnificent stand of cypress across the road. "You'll be looking at 'em. That's the farmhouse where Jack's mother and matriarch of the clan, Cate Dillon, lives along with her grandson, Nate."

"Ah, the mysterious rancher Ava mentioned," Hugo almost smiled. "You know how long it took Ava to get interested in dating? This Nate is a good sign."

"Could be. Look around, get your bearings, Sandoval," T. Ray said before taking the turn.

Two creeks carved their way into the crust of the hillside before chasing each other across the headlands to the sea. Running on either side of the main house, the creeks fed the ranch. Random outbuildings with broken roofs, some with sidewalls lying flat on the ground, appeared to wander at random across the coastal prairie headlands.

Hugo made a note how the old fenceposts leaned and twisted as if they had been set free, their wires trailing in the tall grasses.

Ava's silver bullet Airstream was a gleaming silhouette against the Pacific sunset. "When was the last time you saw your baby girl, Sandoval?" T. Ray wondered as they approached.

Hugo went silent. It had been nine months since he helped his daughter rig up the Flying Cloud for her new position on the coast but all he could picture at that moment was the chattering eight-year-old who used to go on inspections with him, not the woman who now stood outside her trailer, hands on her hips.

Ava had been waiting for them, but the dark green pickup truck threw her. As the distance closed between them, she wondered if a shotgun would have been entirely out of place. She was relieved and happy to hear T. Ray's booming voice as two men alighted from the old cab. Ava ran to her father as if he had just returned from the war, hugging him a little longer than he was used to.

"What's this? You all right, baby?" he asked with concern. He could see she was worn out, but even in that state she was stunning. Ava was the young Carmen, complete with her mother's beautiful, elegant frame and seasoned by Hugo's mixed heritage. Her dark cocoa eyes set off by her skin, the color of spun honey, brought the Cuban in her father to the surface.

T. Ray smothered her in a bear hug, then looked her in the eye. "Ava Rose, what the hell have you been up to? Why haven't you come to see us?"

Ava blushed as her Uncle T kissed her on the forehead.

"Where's Lobo?" Hugo asked. The dog answered with distinct barks from the trailer. Lobo had been Ava's pup since she fled the nest; the 45-pound mutt never left her side. Hugo appreciated loyalty.

"I keep her inside from dusk to dawn; she hates it, but we both hate skunks more."

T. Ray kept on point. "Sun's going down, Rosie; let's have a look at this blue whale of yours."

The beach on the far side of the rocks was in the shadows, but it was hard to miss the leviathan serenely tucked into the rocks below, her head resting on the base of the cliff, her tail dipping into the tidepools.

T. Ray ventured a few feet down the rock face for a better view. He watched as each incoming wave rocked the blue further into her big sleep. A tough guy in most situations, when T. Ray surveyed Chicken Cove he could barely speak. "That's her calf up the beach, on the other side of those rocks? *How*—?"

Backing away from the edge of the cliff, Hugo repositioned his Borsalino against the slight tail of the onshore wind. It had been a long day. Never had he seen anything so pure. Hugo was speechless; tears welled in his eyes.

Long past weeping for the blue and her calf, Ava squeezed her father's hand.

Looking upon the largest creature to ever roam the Earth, the three stood in silent vigil on the cliff. They watched the sun falter and bleed along the horizon cleverly entangled in a sinewy line of fog. It wasn't the beauty of the somber sunset or the taste of the sea air that Hugo would forever remember. It was the defiance of the day to end.

Hugo kept Ava's hand in his as he pondered T. Ray's *how*, but the real question in his mind was *why?*

12

North Coast fog has no rival when it comes to taking the color out of the landscape. Painters soon find they need a palette more expansive than the colors themselves, a palette that comes with a dipping well of sounds borne by a gentle caress from the sea. As Hugo listened to the breaking waves, muffled by four blocks of town and a quarter mile of shoreline, he realized he needed all his senses in play. The reunion with his daughter was vital, but what Hugo had observed over the past four hours could not be ignored.

On a quiet street corner in the coastal lumber town of Fort Bragg, a mismatched pair of herding dogs lay on either side of the revolving doors to the Lost Inn and Pub. Like living stone sentries, the guards remained within earshot of their owner's soft but resonant voice while he tended bar inside. Hugo and T. Ray crossed the empty street to the pub, failing to disturb the tricolor Australian shepherd as he moved closer to the warm wall of the old brick building as the sidewalk cooled. Unimpressed by the unseasonable fog that had swept into town late in the day, the McNab held to his strategic position near the entry, sniffing the go-bag before Hugo entered the inn.

"Sandoval, I wish you would stay with us, at least tonight. If I don't bring you home, Daisy is going to be very unhappy with me."

"You said yourself, the children's wing is all torn up since they flew the coop, but I appreciate the offer. The hotel is best for me, Harrison. It's much closer to Ava and the cove than your hideout in the woods."

"Not to mention closer to the taps. Fitz!" T. Ray called out to the older of the two bartenders. "Meet your guest, Hugo Sandoval."

"*Sláinte*!" boomed the rakish proprietor of the Lost Inn & Pub. After thirty years in the States, Fitz had only lost a bit of his accent

Born in Dublin, Dustin Connor Fitzpatrick celebrated his Irish heritage on the walls and the beer towers of his pub. The original pair of taps still poured light and dark ales and sawdust covered the floors, but Fitz kept up with the times by bringing in local wines and craft beers to keep his patrons happy.

Hugo paid the bill for the night and watched with amusement while the innkeeper tossed the cash into a beat-up drawer beneath the classic mirror on the back bar. The inspector admired the old-school approach.

"Each room comes with a free pint. What can I pour you?" Fitz asked Hugo in his resonant voice as he scrawled the receipt in pencil on an old cardboard pub coaster. "Or maybe you would favor a glass of wine?"

T. Ray muscled in, "We'll have two of the Old Rasputin, Fitz." He turned to Hugo. "This is a true boarding house. You should order something."

Hugo read the chalkboard and recognized a favorite. "Bangers and mash, if the kitchen is still open."

As Fitz put the rich dark beers on the bar, he looked directly at Hugo. "Harry here claims you might be just the man to help me. There's a disability lawsuit hanging over my wee pub." It was almost a challenge.

It took Hugo a second to figure out "Harry" was T. Ray Harrison, III, his associate, and former college football hero.

The barkeep stood his ground for all to hear. "Some fella from *your* city complained he couldn't get through the revolving doors. He's threatening to sue me. I shipped these doors all the way from Cork; been in the family for five generations. I went through hell and back fitting them into that corner, but they work. The county stamped the plans and issued me a permit more than fifteen years ago."

"The man was in a wheelchair, yes?" replied Hugo.

"Indeed, he was," confirmed the pub owner.

"Drive a Chevy Nova? Long ponytail?"

"Yeah, that's exactly right. You know the guy?" asked Fitz, surprised.

"He's a pro," was all that Hugo would say.

Fitz' reaction was odd; he seemed almost relieved to hear the ADA activist was a scammer. Pointing to the far corner of the near empty pub, he called out to a regular—a roguish man in a wheelchair and fisherman's cap.

"Hey, Pally, jump in here," Fitz shouted.

"I would if I could, you old tosser," Pally shouted back. "Look, if it's so damn tough, how did I get in here?"

"Hard for me to say, Pally, hard for me to say, since you were already here when I opened up this morning." Fitz grinned.

"Why don't you show the inspector, Pally," T. Ray threw over his shoulder.

Hugo followed Pally as he wheeled into the men's room, cruised past the urinals, gaining speed enough to push open an unmarked door that led to a caged storage cooler full of beer kegs. In the far wall of the chilly, metal-skinned locker, a set of doors opened to a loading dock.

"Fitz put that in for me," said Pally with a touch of pride as he pointed to a handrail-less plywood ramp that connected the dock to the street level. T. Ray enjoyed the look on Hugo's face when the expedition returned.

Fitz pushed a fresh pint of the settling black liquid on the bar. "Well, Inspector?"

Hugo took a thoughtful sip before reciting, "Reasonable accommodation for equal accessibility to the public and your employees; that's the guideline." Hugo let the line settle before editorializing. "In effect, Fitz, you're asking your mobility-challenged patrons to enter through the men's room—that about right?"

At Otis Street, Hugo was known as a champion of accessibility, but the title was tempered with Hugo's distinct distaste for self-appointed advocates who selfishly turned disabled challenges into a cottage industry. In this case, he sympathized with Fitz.

"Show me around the building tomorrow. Bring a tape measure. Let's see what we can figure out," Hugo said.

"I truly appreciate that, Chief; next one's on me," said Fitz as he reached to answer the bar phone. The barkeep gave the "it's your wife" sign to T. Ray who waved off the call like a catcher at the plate. Fitz abided. "No, Daisy, he's not here. Okay. Okay. Absolutely no trouble. You're welcome, dear. Yes, that *is* exciting. How long will she be? You don't say."

T. Ray quickly emptied his pint glass and was in motion before Fitz cradled the phone. "Sandoval—meet me at the no-name gas station on the highway tomorrow morning before you go see Ava. The station opens at seven," whispered T. Ray as he made his exit.

The Irishman behind the bar patiently pulled a second pint for the inspector, tipping the frosted glass just enough to knock off the foam into the drainboard.

"Harry tells me you're a friend of Nate Dillon," Fitz said.

"A friend of a friend—I've not actually met him yet." Hugo's plate arrived steaming from the kitchen.

"It is a huge thing for the lad, the whale beaching on his ranch like that—well, on his grandmother's ranch. Old Cate Dillon," Fitz smiled. "You'll meet her soon enough; she's a force of nature, that woman. Nothing goes on along her coast she doesn't know about."

Two blokes approached the bar and ordered. Fitz opened the taps and filled a pair of frosted mugs with one hand. Hugo was impressed. After the barman casually tossed their dollars onto the back bar, he returned to his new customer.

Shaking his head in genuine disbelief, "Holy mother, a blue swimming right into Chicken Cove. Of all the places on the coast for her to come to shore. Hell, that gap is no wider than my pub."

With T. Ray gone, Fitz felt it his duty to bring Hugo up to speed on the fishery outside the cove.

"Boundaries are being hashed out in Washington D. C. at this very minute. The groundfish needed to be protected if they're going to survive," the barman explained.

Hugo wondered if *they* meant the fish or the fishing fleet. The tourist dropped back to listen as others at the bar joined in the conversation; more than a few sported stocking caps tightly fitted to their heads. By the time they got around to the declining sea urchin population, Hugo had tuned out. He was stuck on Fitz's choice of words: "swimming right into Chicken Cove."

13

Identified by the absence of brand-name signs or neon or any kind, the gas station on the main drag reflected the independent spirit of the North Coast. Liberated or not, at 7 a.m. on the dot the garage door rolled up to reveal a muscular, balding mechanic suited in overalls with *Ben* stitched in red script over the left breastplate pocket. Hugo was fascinated by the opening ceremony, as the station attendant rolled out the oil can display as if he were spinning his girl on the dancefloor.

The ritual over, the attendant acknowledged his first and only customer with a sharp nod. Hugo, quietly leaning on the 2010 BMW X3 he had parked next to the faceless, grimy white gasoline pump simply labeled SUPER in stick-on reflective letters, nodded back.

"Sir, you're at the self-serve island. You're good there, but let me pump that for you. There's a little hitch to it; confuses the tourists," said the tattooed man in the short-sleeved and machine-pressed Ben Davis pinstripe.

Tourist? He had never been called that before. "Navy man?" Hugo shot back after taking in the USN tattoo on the man's forearm. The design reminded him of the anchor he spotted in the seawall under Pier 50, barely twenty-four hours before, chain and all.

"Ten years," the attendant smiled broadly. "Me and two buddies signed up together right before Desert Storm. This here is my old man's station," he said while the fuel flowed. "I keep it going for him."

T. Ray coasted his truck into the station, cutting the fog like a knife. He could see introductions had gone as well as any with Hugo, so with a good morning to Ben, the investigator passed around fresh coffees from The Joe.

The Navy man enjoyed the early morning company and kept on with his story.

"When I got out, me and my baby brother Andy built kit houses for a couple of years at the mill. Dad was a master millwright then; for forty years, until they shut it down. The three of us lost our jobs the same day. That's when Dad bought the station. Eight-five now and the old man still goes to work every morning. He starts at The Joe, then goes to his woodshop behind the house. Work's work," the veteran smiled. "Mom still packs his lunch just like he was heading off to the mill."

"Ben, you hear anybody wanting to buy the Dillon Ranch?" asked T. Ray.

"Nah, who would want to invest that kind of money around here?" T. Ray and Hugo waited patiently while Ben returned the hose to the pump; he was right, there was a hitch to it.

"The Land Trust people would love to have it, so I hear—but wait, I'm telling *you*?" Ben laughed as he looked at T. Ray. "You could have heard something in the wind, but with the recession hanging around like an old fart and the damn mill site putting all of us at each other's throats as to what to do with it, I can't see why developers would even look twice at the Dillon Ranch. Ray, your own wife could have told you that much. One thing I do know, if Cate does sell, it will be for some serious cash. She's nobody's fool."

Hugo had drifted away from the pumps without paying, leaving it to T. Ray to settle up. The local pulled out cash for the gas and a little extra for the information that was about to pay off.

As T. Ray turned to go, Ben held him up. "All these rumors about developing this or restoring that don't mean shit to most of us. You know all this. You might have your feet in two puddles but you're one of us, Ray." Ben paused to think. "Time is just eating us down to the bone, but I know a way we could survive if we had any balls."

T. Ray bit the flashy lure. "Pot?"

"Hell, yeah, pot. That's good money but only if you've got the land. No, I'm talking about harvesting a new crop out in the sanctuary." Ben lowered his voice. "You heard about the sunken logs off the point, right? And not just logs—milled timber. Any chance your wife could help me get a permit to go get 'em? The conservation folks have decreed that pulling them up will disturb the precious marine habitat. Horseshit! Ray, there is a gold mine out there not even fifty feet down, I'm tellin' ya. Put half the town back work. Where's the concern about *our* habitat?"

T. Ray had heard about the logs; in fact he was certain everybody in town knew the story. Over the years, the tales had taken on a mythical quality. "Fort Bragg's Buried Treasure"—he could see the brochures now. The trouble was no one knew exactly where the logs were located or how many there were out there resting on the shelf. Besides, if they existed at all they would be sitting in the protected waters of the marine sanctuary and in deep water.

"Come up to the house sometime; bring your wife. Hell, bring that guy!" Ben chuckled as he looked to Hugo who had walked to the dune fence behind the station.

"Sure, we'll drop by sometime; it would be good to see your mother again," said T. Ray "It's been too long. But Ben, I'm not sure Daisy can help with the permit idea. If anything, the sanctuary is expanding, and the coastal zone will be even more off limits than it is now. I can't see her signing on. Besides, you don't even know where to look."

"Yeah, I hear ya, but what if I did? What if I *knew* where to look? That might convince her, yeah?"

T. Ray was curious.

"Dad worked at the mill for forty years before they let us all go. When they were shutting it down, the old man came across box of old docking slips from the early 1900s. He keeps them out in his workshop. A little piece of history, he calls it.

T. Ray looked around to get a fix on Hugo, who had disappeared out of sight.

Ben held onto his story. "The mill was buying logs from closed mills as far north as the Lost Coast. Lumber prices crashed in the 1920s and mills were going under right and left but Union Lumber here was buying. Written on each docking slip is the name of the ship and number of logs delivered to the mill. We forgot about those mill tags until last spring when Mom came home from St. Michael's jumble with an old trunk. Leather hinges, canvas-covered, in bad shape overall. She thought it would be a good project for Dad 'cuz he likes restoring stuff."

"I'm not following you, Ben."

"The trunk was full of ship manifests. Some of the manifests are from the same ships listed on the mill's docking slips stored in the loft of Dad's workshop." Ben waited for T. Ray to catch on. "You following me now?"

Like a bell at the end of a round, it dawned on him. "The numbers don't match," said T. Ray.

Ben beamed. "Some do but there are dozens of dates where the log count delivered is short of what was picked up at the ports up the coast. Thousands of logs went overboard before they were delivered, Ray, and today they're still sitting on the bottom of the Pacific waiting for someone to come back for them."

"Doesn't make sense. Why would a captain deliberately dump part of his cargo?" asked T. Ray.

"Hard to say. The mill was notorious back then for not paying for a full load either to the ship or to the small mills up the coast but who the hell knows?" Ben said a little bitterly. "Some history books even say the ships dumped the extra logs, came back empty to the mill to pick up cut lumber bound for San Francisco which paid better. Hell, half the Pacific is a dumping ground, fuel, garbage, even radioactive waste." Ben editorialized. "It took a little math and navigation, but we're close to figuring out exactly where those logs were sent to the bottom. I can't put it on a chart for you just yet, but let's say I can almost spit to where some were chucked over the side."

"It's a risk if you just go for it, Ben."

"I'm tellin' you flat out, if this recession doesn't ease up a bit, me and my little brother are going timber-fishing, and trust me, we won't be the only boat out there."

T. Ray caught up to Hugo at the fence between the station and the open coast. "You owe me forty-three bucks," he said. "For the gas *and* the scoop."

Hardly just a dune fence anymore, the six-foot-high chain link was capped with another twelve inches of barbed wire coiled on top since Georgia Pacific took ownership of the mill site. In the distance, the restricted shoreline of Fort Bragg covering six miles of pristine shoreline was littered with decommissioned lumber mill buildings, polluted ponds, and unpaid pensions symbolically buried in the contaminated dunes. All in, four hundred and fifteen acres of a magnificent Pacific coastline locked in, completely off limits to the town.

"Remind you of anything, Harrison?" asked Hugo thinking of his hometown waterfront.

"Yeah, looks a little like that spot in China Basin." Both he and Hugo hated those long stretches of the San Francisco waterfront that remained fenced off from the people although more than a few had found holes in the fence—the homeless, the curious, along with ordinary citizens wanting to fish or simply walk along the shoreline. Hugo grabbed the chain link as if to test the strength of the fence around the old mill site. He concluded it was formidable.

"I live with this, Sandoval," T. Ray said, a bit nostalgically, looking over the wasteland. "Daisy has worked for years to open up this coastline, but Georgia Pacific has been one nasty adversary."

"So, what was that all about sunken logs?"

"Sandoval, your hearing is just plain spooky."

"I've told you before, it's all about concentration, Harrison." Hugo reminded him.

"Seriously, what's with the logs?" Hugo wanted to know.

"Very hot market right now for *sinkers*. Logs mostly, or milled lumber that's been sitting on the bottom for a hundred years in cold water, no oxygen. Beautiful grains, long straight runs from old-growth trees."

Hugo nodded as he fielded a barrage of texts from Otis Street. From the looks of it, Sara had been busy. Abstracted from an *LA Times* article from September 2002, Hugo's 'No. 1' had added bullets below the headline, "Fort Bragg Faces Loss Of Lumber Mill."

- *timber industry blames both government and environmental lawsuits*
- *environmentalists blame the industry and the mill for poor timber management*
- *GP boasted a payroll of 2000 at its peak*
- *mill lays off the last 125 locals—many in sight of retirement*
- *"Just like the dinosaurs, we've become extinct," says laid-off millworker, Ben Davis, Sr.*

"This gas guy. Is his name really Ben Davis?"

"Junior," said T. Ray.

"Small town."

"You don't know the half of it, Sandoval. "

It was time for T. Ray to explain the economy of the North Coast, or rather the lack of.

"You've got to appreciate how tough these people are. Fort Bragg had all the earmarks of a company town built in the 1880s by the innovative Union Lumber Company."

"Unionized?"

"Nah, but *progressive* in its day. Lumber mills in that era straddled almost every river drainage on the North Coast. Today, there are maybe four still in operation. Georgia Pacific picked this one up in 1972. After 9/11, the Koch Brothers closed the mill for good. It was a kidney punch to the town without a doubt, but keep in mind the tenacity of these people. Fort Bragg had already been in survivor mode with the fishing industry in deep trouble for more than a decade; it still is, for that matter. But as tough as these folks have proven to be, when this recession hit two years ago, it washed away the last hopes for a lot of the families up here."

"And this sunken timber, it's valuable?"

"Oh, yeah, extremely valuable, that is, if they can get permission to bring them up. The old-growth redwood alone would be worth the dive. Until this morning I would have said it was all academic, but Ben just changed my mind." T. Ray said. "I believe the Davis boys could pull it off, legal or not."

"It's all very interesting, but what does this have to do with Ava's whale?" Hugo asked.

After furiously rubbing his mop of gray-streaked, straw-colored curls, T. Ray added, "Ben said a funny thing just now. He told me that all it would take would be a phone call to any one of a handful of fishing boat captains for him and his brother to suit up." He waited for his comment to sink in. "That's a voice of desperation, Chief."

"Is our friend Skip on that list?"

"He didn't name names." T. Ray handed Hugo a small brown paper bag. "This might be nothing, but I thought you should see it."

Hugo solemnly opened the bag. Inside, the plastic-framed news clipping from the wall at The Joe. Bella had been curious but hadn't questioned why T. Ray had wanted to borrow it. He figured she might already have some idea.

"You know where you are—and where you have to turn for Ava?"

Hugo nodded.

"I got a couple of loose ends to track down. I'll catch up with you later at City Hall. Two o'clock, right?" Hugo nodded again. "And Sandoval, don't forget, you owe me forty-three bucks,"T. Ray shouted over his shoulder to Hugo still leaning on the fence, the clipping hanging from his good hand.

Inside the fence, stacks of milled lumber floated on the broken tarmacs, their dreams like the town's, abandoned.

What had his Ava gotten into? he asked the onshore wind as it kicked up and set loose the corrugated panels on the back of the old gas station.

14

MORNINGS ON THE HEADLANDS can be a cool drink of water at the end of a long night. It was in that muted light Ava walked her father along the overgrown footpath skirting the bluff. As the trail led away from the Cove, Hugo entered the quiet of the coastal forest. He had found his daughter determined, even stronger than he remembered, and was eager to meet this new man in her life who, only minutes away, was cooking them breakfast in a red-tagged beach cottage.

Lobo was intent on herding Hugo who often lagged behind picking up his own trails. When Hugo explored foreign soil, he needed to stop occasionally to take it all in—trees that seemed to sprout like wheat, sudden ear-piercing cries from the canopy, and the strange, seductive smell of a woodfire growing stronger as they neared the clearing.

Lobo nipped at his hip as if to say, "Keep moving, Dad." The mutt was eager to catch up to Ava who had already climbed on the deck of the beach cottage and was standing close to a tall, sun-weathered young man. Despite the pup's encouragement, Hugo stopped again to take in a full rendering of the cottage that he was told his host used as an art studio. He wished Harrison had joined him; this he had to see.

The Dillon outpost was a far cry from the toothy farm shacks that randomly dotted the aging coastal farms. Hugo was surprised. Before him rose an intimate modern structure completely in tune with the headlands. He admired its confident perch not thirty yards from the point which dropped to the thundering Pacific below. Hugo would comment later that the beach cottage was not as much *built* as it was *woven* into the landscape. He loved how the roofline tucked into the lilting Monterey cypress and pines that defied the North Coast winds.

"He does that sometimes," Ava whispered to Nate, and giggled nervously.

"Does what?" he whispered back, his gaze lingering on the woman next to him.

"That." Ava nodded in the direction of her father who circled the cottage. Ava was oddly comforted by the ritual. "As Mother would say, there's no cause for concern, he's just marking his territory," and the girl laughed her mother's laugh. Nate was slow to turn away from her but, when he did, he watched a man who appeared to be touring a gallery, surveying the art from all angles.

Lobo jumped off the deck to corral Hugo, close enough for Ava to reach down and drag her father up the steps to the deck before he could take another tour. Hugo cautiously side-stepped around the piles of driftwood and shore finds to shake the young man's hand. He had already begun to make mental notes of Nate Dillon: early twenties, fit, deep blue eyes that didn't waver on contact. *Solid* is the word he would use if he were to tell his ex-wife about meeting Nate at the beach cottage.

"You caught me on moving day, Mr. Sandoval. Gran wants me to move my art studio to the farmhouse," said the artist. "The whale on her doorstep has her all upset. It's bringing strangers onto the property, news people and photographers. Gran likes her privacy."

Hugo took it all in—the coffee, his finds and driftwood from the beach drying, the seasoned forest floor surrounding the cottage, and Ava, her face tired but radiant, hopeful. "Please, call me Hugo."

It had been a long time since the City boy had eaten a meal cooked on a wood-burning stove. The smells brought back happy memories of his mother cooking on a potbelly in their tiny house on the Greenwich Steps. Ava took the stage and chattered on about the whale while the men ate eggs, fishcakes, and a last-minute grab from Nate's grandmother's pie safe, wild grape pie. Although the coffee had been slightly burnt, it was well-suited to the meal. Hugo enjoyed himself immensely and complimented Nate on a wall-mounted sculpture made entirely of driftwood.

"It's a self-portrait," Nate explained. Hugo simply nodded, struggling to see the resemblance.

Ava would never have described her father as distant or removed in any way, just unique. She knew his heart was there for her, and for her mother, but she also knew he was passionately protective of his City. While some thought Hugo was obsessed, Ava was in awe of his dedication. She, for one, was willing to share him with the people who had no other recourse than to turn to him for help. She was heartbroken when she learned her mother had grown tired of such sharing.

That morning at the Dillon beach cottage, Ava recognized her father's characteristic drift and called him back. "Nate is a sculptor, Dad. He builds art out of salvage he finds in the woods or on the beach." Ava proudly pointed to one of the more figurative assemblages of bark and driftwood. "Like that one."

Of all Hugo's passions, art was high on the list, and he found himself drawn to Nate Dillon's natural constructions.

"But getting back to the blue, Dad. Every research lab and museum wants a piece of her." She launched into her second piece of grape pie. "My team will have harvested what organs we can salvage by the end of the day. A New Zealand institute has asked that the eyes be transported in solution. Can you imagine? And there is a lab in Iceland requesting her heart be flash frozen and shipped overnight. Iceland, Dad; it's absolutely nuts—the whale's heart is the size of a small car. Thankfully, the director of the Academy of Sciences fields the requests—even the crazy ones, but at this point it's all about what we can preserve for further study." Ava carefully wrapped the remainder of the pie in a dishtowel as precious as one of the rare whale's organs.

"How often does this happen?" asked her empathetic father.

"More and more unfortunately. The sea is changing. The abnormally warm waters are bringing the krill in close and she's right behind them. It's rare for a blue whale to calve this far north. Probably on her way to Baja to give birth but sadly she swam right through a shipping lane. It's not her fault. She must have been following the food. We gotta slow down the ships."

Ava suddenly sounded tired. "Satellites have been tracking blue whales off the West Coast for years. The lanes need to be moved but today, today my problem is Aunt Daisy. Dad, she wants the skeleton of the mother blue; she wants it bad. She thinks she can get the town to build a museum around it. The director of the Academy is considering her plan and is flying up but I'm not so sure we can get the skeleton out of the Cove before the high tides. I tried to warn her, but you know Aunt Daisy—once she's in gear, she takes things to a whole other level. She already has the Yurok tribe sending their chief whale hunter down from Humboldt along with a tribal elder to perform a ceremony Sunday morning."

"Just do your work; don't worry about disappointing Daisy. I'll talk to Harrison, but he'll meet the same wall," said Hugo, scraping up the last of his pie.

"You see, the trouble is the blubber," Nate jumped in. "Ava estimates there's as much as 80 tons of it. Even if she can safely remove the flesh, the blubber must be transported off the beach, up the cliff before it can be hauled away to be processed. Blue whales are a protected species under the Marine Mammal Protection Act which takes commercial harvesting of the blubber off the table."

"It's considered poaching," Ava added, looking at her cell phone. "We're out of range out here; I should go back soon, Dad."

"It's a federal crime," added Nate.

Hugo thought how harvesting the sunken lumber would have the same logistical problem. "I get that."

"Let me show you how this happens," Ava said. She scrolled through some rather gory details of flensing the carcass while Nate pulled up his photographs of the actual rotting whale, many with Ava in them.

"Have you figured out what happened to her?" Hugo pushed away his plate, his appetite lost.

"Propeller probably. See where this cut is?" Ava pointed to one of the photographs on Nate's phone. "The gash is almost eight feet long. It nearly severed the spinal cord but somehow, she kept swimming." Ava was visibly upset just talking about it. "I spoke to the captain of the ship, the *Sea Star*. He said he was about seven miles out on the edge of a canyon when he felt the shudder." She paused to control her emotions. "She was heading south to calve in another month or so."

"How big a ship?" Hugo felt a little queasy after the graphic flensing photos.

"Almost twice as long as Grace," Nate responded.

"The irony is that this ship was full of scientists hired by the NOAA to map the seafloor. With those maps, they will be able to designate the habitats to be included in the sanctuary," Ava added. "They were there to make it *safer* for the whales."

"You named her Grace," noted the inspector.

"My mother's name," Nate said quietly. "Ava said since I found her, I'm the one to name her."

Hugo recognized the sadness in Nate's voice and it translated to his daughter's face.

She cares for him, he thought; he wasn't expecting that.

"Was Grace swimming with her calf into the cove?" asked Hugo thinking about what Fitz had said.

"The umbilical cord is still attached to the calf. Ava thinks the calf was born in the cove," Nate answered.

"Amazing. Are all their calves white at birth?" Hugo wondered aloud.

"Hard to say," said Ava softly. "No one's ever seen one born before."

It was impossible not to detect the hushed thrill in his daughter's voice. Sadly, the wild beeping of Ava's cell phone broke the spell, "Ah, I've got to take this!"

With an apologetic look to Nate and a grape pie kiss planted on her father's head, Ava rushed back to her Airstream command post with Lobo.

When just the two of them were left in Nate's little cottage, Hugo asked his host, "The whale is fascinating, it is, but that's not why I'm here, is it, Nate?"

15

NATE WASHED THE DISHES while Hugo observed the moon-shaped chips in the white-scoured drainboard; he wondered how many meals had been run over those porcelain ribs. After the artist dried his hands on his flannel shirttail, he opened the cupboard next to the farmhouse sink and pulled out a beat-up envelope.

"I found this the night before last. Ava wanted me to speak to you about it right away. She said it's your thing," and handed the red tag to Hugo.

Although sleeved in plastic, the notice had been severely water stained. The bold lettering survived clearly, "Substandard Building, DO NOT ENTER Unsafe to Occupy," while the rest of the red tag was blurred. Hugo copied the details into a text and photographed both sides of the red tag to send to Otis Street as soon as he got back into cell phone range.

"There would be a complaint filed along with this. Were you served any papers?"

Nate sat down heavily at the kitchen table across from Hugo. "Not sure if we were or not. You see, Mr. Sandoval, I'm not the owner of the ranch. My Gran is. When I took this to her, she didn't mention any complaint, but I can tell you that Gran was as upset as I have ever seen her and I'm not exactly sure why. It's hard to describe but it's just not the way she typically responds to things. Even at her age, Gran can handle most matters, but something about the whale has put her on edge, as I said before. And I don't exactly know what."

Hugo had been taking in the feel of the beach cottage. It was as if the years had not made their mark—the furnishings were sparse, a futon couch, no TV, few photos, and the detailed Craftsman bookcases had just a few magazines; it was as if the books had been removed. In contrast to the cottage, the contents were almost impersonal.

"Nate, do you live out here alone?"

"Yeah, since the summer. I moved up here after Dad was killed."

"I heard about that. I'm sorry for your loss."

"Thanks." Nate shook off the condolences and said defiantly, "There's nothing wrong with this house. My father built it when I was a kid. He might not have been a great rancher, but he was a fine carpenter; he could build anything." Nate's voice wavered.

Even holding it up to the light, Hugo could barely make out the deputy's name on the red tag. "A. Ruiz, Badge #402. Know him?"

Nate shook his head.

"Did you call the sheriff's office?"

"Ava asked me the same question, but it's not that simple."

"Complicated?" Hugo helped him out.

"Yeah. Exactly that," he said quietly, stopping short of an explanation.

The boy had placed his hands palms down on the table, fingers spread wide. Hugo studied his hands as if the hands, not Nate, were weighing the question.

Finally, Nate rose. "What the hell. Come look at this."

The building inspector had already noticed the missing thresholds and gaps in the floorboards—what next?

Nate led Hugo to a locked closet under the staircase to the loft.

Inside were a dozen rifles: military, shotguns and .22s.

Nate confessed, "When I moved in after the accident, I found them in every corner of the house. All loaded. All of them."

"What was your father afraid of?"

"I only wish I knew," said Nate.

"What does your gran think?"

"It was too weird. I didn't tell her because she would have freaked out." Nate shut the closet door and leaned against it.

Hugo was moved by the young man. Where some might see a sadness in his eyes, he saw a strength bonded with a tenderness, a caring for his grandmother, he hoped extended to Ava.

He recalled what Harrison had advised after the rendezvous with Ava the night before. "Leave the City behind and let your daughter show you her world in her own time." *Good advice*, Hugo thought, *but fat chance now.*

Hugo knew Ava had a full plate just with the whale, but he wondered how well she had known Nate before her whale found his ranch. What were the odds? He knew it was important not to overreact as a father and he would try to keep emotions at bay. He determined it was best to proceed as if it were any other case crossing his desk at Otis Street, but it wasn't. He had been on the Coast less than twenty-four hours, and despite solid support from his team, he was seriously considering calling Carmen. But he would have to think about that later.

Hugo added the new observations from the cottage to his internal checklist, or what Harrison liked to call his *infernal* checklist:

- *thresholds and floorboards disturbed*
- *loaded guns; stashed*
- *Dillon's father—paranoid or threatened?*
- *red tag; no discernable violations*
- *grandmother's reaction to whale*

While Nate loaded a small wagon with tools and beach finds to take to the farmhouse, Hugo inspected the front door to the beach cottage. He appreciated the restored Victorian five-panel; it was a simple but elegant addition to the modern cottage and fit nicely. The door was complete with its original 1880s Eastlake hinges, knobs, and skeleton-key lock, all true to the Victorian period, no doubt in tribute to the original farmhouse. The redwood door was quite possibly salvaged from one of the older buildings on the ranch; he would ask Cate Dillon. But what did *not* fit also caught the eye of the building inspector: the modern deadbolt.

"I'd like to meet your gran," Hugo turned to Nate. "I should have some answers for you about the red tag after lunch."

"She would like that. Thanks."

"And I'd like to bring my friend along; maybe Ava's told you about him? T. Ray Harrison? He's my investigator."

"Sure! I've heard a lot about Uncle T," Nate smiled.

"Nate, tell me, how do you two know each other? You and my Ava?"

Maneuvering the cart through the forest, Nate's smile was restored at the mention of her name and was eager to tell the story.

"I was exhibiting my work at her marine lab. It was a benefit for the marine mammal rescue program back in March. I must confess, your daughter is the main reason I moved back to the ranch. Until I met her, I had been living in Southern California, in a little beach town,"

"Hermosa Beach," Hugo interrupted.

"She told you?"

"No. You're famous," he said. "I saw the newspaper clipping."

Nate blushed. "Notoriety more than fame, I'd call it."

"Tell me, what's it like to ride a house down a cliff?

As Hugo listened to Nate's tale, he turned on the path a few times to look back at the beach cottage.

Cleverly built upon redwood stumps, the cottage had been constructed of redwood with a little Doug fir for tenacity, and a touch of what he suspected was madrone, for beauty. *Arbutus menziesii*,

Pacific madrone. One of Hugo's mentors, Lawrence Halprin, the visionary landscape architect with whom he shared a love of vernacular structures—*those born of the environment in which they are built*, would have been pleased with Hugo's Latin recall. Halprin would have loved to hear of a beach cottage adorned with the scaly bark of those twisted buttery-russet trees native to the forests of the North Coast. But if the student remembered correctly, Pacific madrone were not common at sea level which made Hugo wonder about the height of the coastal hills rising behind the farmhouse.

In addition to loving the timber skin of the cottage, which had been left to age naturally, Hugo was taken with the single accent, the blood-red paint. Besides the red on the front door, the paint had been splashed across the sliding barn doors facing the Pacific. While the footing of the cottage deliberately tucked into the trees ultimately protected the isolated dwelling from exposure to the elements, it was the sliders that provided the ultimate defense. Hugo admired how the ingenious design of the sliding doors allowed flexibility to open the outpost to the elements or close tight as storms threatened from the often-unruly seacoast.

Beyond the impressive structure, Hugo found it was the red paint that transformed and even branded the sullen outpost.

Still in mourning over the recent death of his mentor, Hugo continued to be inspired by Halprin's understanding of the collision of the natural habitat with the built environment. The architect had often used the word *collision,* which was stuck in Hugo's head as he walked the headlands of the Dillon Ranch with Nate. He could see ideas had collided at the beach cottage and wondered if it had anything to do with the red tag.

In Hugo's eyes, the construction of the beach cottage suggested a far more intimate connection with the sea than to the world its builder had left behind. As he followed the carpenter's son toward the Airstream where Ava was at work, Hugo was beginning to understand the man who built his refuge on a cliff.

The red-tagged structure was solid, the location safe, albeit close to the cliffs and it had been constructed more than twenty years before in a remote corner of a private ranch—completely off the grid—so, the question remained, why would anyone care? Why the red tag? Even more disturbing, why the guns, the broken floorboards, the missing thresholds, and now, the need for a deadbolt? The building inspector's internal checklist was growing at an alarming rate. Reluctantly, he added the "red on the barn doors" to the list.

Was it a mark of passion—or distress?

16

WHEN HUGO SHOWED UP AT THE RANCH for breakfast that morning, the only other vehicle parked near the Airstream had been Nate's truck. By ten o'clock, the parking lot had changed. Some 246 miles from San Francisco and Bay Area gridlock, Hugo found it odd to be stuck in a traffic jam while trying to leave the ranch. The blue whale and her calf on the beach at Chicken Cove had attracted a cluster of public safety agencies which had inadvertently sealed off access from the ranch headlands to the coast road. While uniforms sorted it out, Hugo felt the rented BMW automatically engage the all-wheel drive feature as he threaded between park police, sheriff cars, and highway patrol vehicles scattered across the pasture.

The slow pace allowed Hugo to continue his conversation with Nate, who walked alongside the car on the lookout for ruts and rocks.

"I gave the sheriff the run of the ranch, but the cliffs are still a worry," he told Hugo. "Ava thinks this might get out of control with the public wanting to get a close look at the whales. I figure once the press shows up, it's game over."

"I think they're already here," said Hugo through his side window. "I hope your liability insurance is paid up." Nate's handsome face was creased with worry.

"I'll have to check with Gran about that. Thing is, my family doesn't own the beach. Twenty-five feet inland from the shoreline is state property. As I see it, the whales are their problem."

Hugo couldn't help but recall the story Alfred Kleinen told him only the morning before. How much more difficult it would be to push a whale back into the sea than the dead human body Al was forced to return to the Bay. If the captain of the *Tango II* was to be believed, the research vessel that hit the blue tried to cover her tracks by towing her out sea in the dark of night. Hugo knew someone had tried but he doubted if it was the research vessel.

In the clearing short of turning onto the highway, Hugo stopped the car. He could see Nate was frustrated, even angry.

"Look, my family has been working this farm for more than a hundred years, and it's been a fight since day one to make a living off this land. We pay for insurance and property taxes, taxes to keep the fire roads clear, taxes to restore the creeks," he stopped himself. "I just figure, now it's their turn."

Ah, there it is—there's the Irish in the lad, Hugo smiled to himself.

Nate was embarrassed. "I shouldn't go on like that. I'm just worried about my grandmother; she could get hurt. You see Gran is fanatical about her afternoon constitutional to the weather station; she likes to go alone. Yesterday, she allowed me to walk with her if I would show her the whale but today, she told me she'd go it alone. I can see that today is going to be wild. Gran's tough, but she's still an old woman."

"What kind of weather station?" asked Hugo intrigued.

"It's not much more than a wooden hut perched on legs standing on the chaparral," Nate said, holding his arms out, "about yo-big. It sits on the beach side of the highway. The ranch has kept records at the station since 1930. Every day at 4 o'clock, Gran walks through the tunnel under the highway, then climbs the path to the weather station. She records the high and low temperatures and rainfall in her notebook, then heads back to the farmhouse and phones in her report. Gran's an important part of the national weather network," he added proudly. "She even keeps a couple of local radio stations informed. Wait, if you get out here, you can almost see it from here." Nate pointed toward the westside opening of the tunnel under the highway.

Hugo was distracted by movement in his side view mirror. A man and a small child had breached the perimeter and were approaching the cliff not far from where he had stood with Harrison and Ava the night before.

Nate was right. It was going to be a wild day on the ranch.

Tourists.

17

FALLOUT FROM FRIDAY'S SHOTGUN PRESS CONFERENCE on Pier 50 continued to land on Sara's desk at Otis Street. She flagged Saturday morning's headlines which read, "Watchdog Challenges Government Agencies" and "Port Developers to Act on Sea Level Rise." Despite sea level rise being her baby, Sara decided to let both accolades and accusations sit over the weekend until the inspector returned to the office Monday morning.

By asking Sara to keep her phone on through the weekend, Hugo revealed his anxiousness in leaving the City to find Ava. He knew that when she was away from Otis Street, Sara dedicated her time to her family but somehow always remained available to her chief. It only took one night on the North Coast before he sent his first message to his consummate assistant.

6:45 a.m. / locate all mortgages, liens, loans on the Dillon Ranch outside of Fort Bragg. —HS.

That extracurricular request would take Sara some time to track down and he was eager for her to get an early start. Sara was unrivaled in investigative research and had well earned her nickname at Otis Street, *No. 1.* When her research gear was engaged, Sara was incomparable—part librarian, part savant. T. Ray referred to it as her "search and destroy" gear.

Hugo sent texts to her throughout the day whenever he could find a connection.

8:15 a.m. / how frequently are blue whales hit by ships? —HS

Almost immediately she shot back,

8:21 a.m. / 1,800 blues on West Coast; unknown # of strikes but increasing due to food supply luring deep water whales into shipping lanes; download Ship Finder app—SD

Breakfast at the beach cottage over, he sent,

8:22 a.m. / background on Nathanial Dillon? —HS

To field that one, Sara relied on a journalist at the *San Francisco Chronicle* who owed her a favor.

10:15 a.m. / Nathaniel Dillon / b. August 13, 1990 / Mendocino Coast District Hospital, BFA National College of Art & Design, Dublin 2010 / Artist in Residence, Headlands Center for the Arts, Sausalito 2011 / North Coast Marine Laboratory Special Exhibition, Bodega Bay 2011 — SD

Hugo thrived on her texts, but it was Sara's reply to the first early morning request that caused him to question her findings—which he did rarely, if ever. The news that the Dillon Ranch was owned free and clear surprised him.

11:45 a.m. / repeat: locate all mortgages, liens, loans on the Dillon Ranch—HS

11:52 a .m / sorry Chief, confirmed. Dillon Ranch free + clear. sending you full report via email —SD

It was a shocker. Sara's detailed report of public tax records showed that the huge delinquent property taxes on the ranch had been paid off in July. No liens, not even an old farm loan popped up. How had the 714 acres of the Dillon Ranch suddenly become so liquid? A final text that morning delivered even more shocking news.

11:55 a.m. / Chief—expect incoming; Ava's mother + Cal Sciences honchos via USN helicopter —SD

12:15 p.m. / don't mess with me, No. 1—HS

Sara enjoyed a rare and golden equilibrium between her private and public life. Dave, her husband of fifteen years, was a bar pilot who guided ships in and out of the San Francisco Bay at all hours while her boss for the last ten-plus years *never* left the city limits—well, not until that weekend, anyway.

A tad piqued that Hugo questioned her earlier findings, Sara was tempted to turn off her cell and take her kids to the movies. Instead, she plugged the device into the charger and texted her husband that she needed his help; the story up the coast was just about to get interesting.

12:16 p.m. / did the Sea Star go back for the whale? —HS

12:18 p.m. / did the Sea Star see any other boats on the water that night? —HS

12:19 p.m. / where is the Sea Star now? —HS

18

WHEN HUGO ARRIVED IN DOWNTOWN FORT BRAGG, T. Ray's Chevy was not alone in front of City Hall. A cerulean blue Volvo station wagon had snuggled-up into a reserved slot near a cast iron lamppost. The sign on the lamppost read, RESERVED FOR MAYOR.

Hugo stared at the redwood two-story Craftsman which owed its character to the vibrant lumber town. Originally built as a community center in 1921, the magnificent Fort Bragg City Hall defined what a public building should be, at least to Hugo. As he peered through the locked front entry to the main floor, he saw reflections of the glory days of the Redwood Empire when the coastal village had been anointed the company town for the mighty Union Lumber Company. In his walk around the structure, Hugo peered through windows, many still glazed with the original wavy glass, to inspect several rooms on the first floor roped off with yellow caution tape. He hoped it was just a restoration and not an attempt to modernize the building. As he entered the building through a side door, he anticipated creaky wooden floorboards, drafty offices shooting off noisy corridors, overpainted wainscotings, and granite toilet stalls inside restrooms wrapped in subway tile walls over little quarter-sized white hexagon floor tiles. Hugo was not disappointed.

To top it off, the unexpectedly ornate ceramic water fountain next to the rear stairwell caused the seasoned inspector to take a deep involuntary breath. Hugo was in love.

"Harrison, I should work here. It's time I quit Otis Street; I've had a good run," he said, half-serious. "Harrison, are you listening?"

T. Ray ignored his friend's exuberance, choosing instead to take long strides down the hall to the mayor's office where he found Mayor Eli Callaghan seated behind an enormous desk. The mayor had just hung up on the Feds and was eager to vent when he saw T. Ray. But as soon as Hugo entered, Eli jumped out of his chair to greet the inspector.

"Apologies, Chief. I'm usually calmer than this, you can ask Ray. It's just swell to finally meet you. I know you only arrived last night, but your reputation has been here for some time now." The mayor smiled broadly.

Hugo figured his grin alone could get the man elected, while the handshake was icing on the cake.

"I'm sure you've heard about our illegal weed grows up here?"

Hugo conceded, "Harrison filled me in."

"Everywhere you look, renegade grows are taking over. You should see the piles of trash leftover when they're finished growing." Eli shook his head, lamenting the fate of his county. "I call it bycatch. It's polluting the streams, clogging up the ravines—it's a goddamned hydra. As soon as you clean up one, another one springs up down the road." He tapped his pencil nervously on the desk.

"Took me two months to get the Feds out there, but they waited to raid the crop until right before harvest—just like the poachers; makes you wonder." Eli cracked. "The black-suited raiders were happy to haul off the cannabis plants, but they left behind all the trappings they confiscated at the tender's camp: irrigation pipes, pesticides, tents, you name it—mountains of bycatch. I called the sheriff to come out and look; after all, it's his jurisdiction.

"Don't get me wrong, Chief, I sympathize with the job they're asked to do, it's the worst. These bootleg farms are everywhere—on private land, in the national forests, and it is getting damned dangerous. This year so far, we've had five homicides in the county because of these grows; one of the shootings took one of our own."

"Finally, the sheriff sends a deputy out to investigate the grow on my land. The result?" Eli tossed a paper to T. Ray and explained to Hugo, "I get fined $250 for an illegal dumpsite on my own property!"

T. Ray had heard the story before, but this was the first he heard the kicker. He burst into laughter. Hugo recalled that the Harrisons and the Callaghans had been neighbors for years.

"The deputy sheriff you spoke with wasn't Ruiz, was it?" Hugo asked.

"No, but I know Andy. He part of this?" The mayor asked, sounding surprised.

"I filled in Eli about the basics when I got home last night." T. Ray explained to his boss.

Hugo slid the red tag from the Dillons' beach house across the desk to the mayor.

Reviewing the notice, the mayor looked troubled. "Yep, that would be Andy Ruiz, all right. After what Ray told me last night, I called the sheriff first thing. So far, he hasn't been able to locate the complaint. That's very strange. Look, Chief, I don't want you to think you landed in some backwater town. While the ranch is over the county line and outside my jurisdiction, I promise I'll get to the bottom of this. Look, the sheriff's on his way over now. You're more than welcome to stick around," Eli sat back in his desk chair.

"What are you thinking, Chief?" T. Ray nudged him. The allure of the swivel seat, lower back padding, and wide arms of the 1920s banker's chair Eli occupied momentarily distracted Hugo.

"Sounds like you're doing all you can, and we do appreciate it," Hugo said to Eli, nodding to T. Ray.

"What hits me funny, fellas, is why anyone would even know the cottage was out on those cliffs—unless they're from around here?" Eli added. "You've seen the location. There's a locked gate and a cattle guard to cross. All you see from the road is a clump of trees. Doesn't make sense. Chief, what do you think could be wrong with it?"

"Nothing that I could see but I want to take Harrison back with me. Maybe you could tell me about its builder? Harrison said you knew Jack Dillon."

Eli paused to sort through memories. "Sure. The only thing is, where to begin." Hugo could see the mayor's boyish exuberance droop suddenly as he remembered his history with the Dillons, especially with Jack. When he found his bearings, it was the rasp in Eli's voice that made Hugo clear his own throat.

"I knew Jack well. We were good friends growing up; played football in high school together. Jesus, Jack was helluva craftsman, could build anything, but he was no farmer. Being the only son of a farmer, especially the son of Big J.D., well, that was a problem for Jack. The Dillons ranched sheep, cows, beef cattle, just about everything that could survive out there. When J.D. died, Jack closed the dairy and enlisted in the Marines. A couple of us went along. We trained down in San Diego. That's where Jack met Grace on a furlough and married her like that." He snapped his fingers.

"Jack went to Desert Storm. When he shipped out, Grace came up here to live at the ranch with Cate. Eighteen months later, the Marines sent Jack home. Honorable discharge. He was in one piece but not *whole*, if you know what I mean." Eli sipped the last of his cold coffee.

"That's when Jack built the beach cottage out on the cliff. He built it for *her*."

"You weren't in the war, were you, Eli?" T. Ray confirmed.

"No, no, I was sent home from boot camp. They figured I had one too many concussions playing football and the next one might get somebody killed."

"And Grace?" asked Hugo.

"Ah, Grace," Eli's tone softened. "Sweet, beautiful gal, eyes the color of cornflowers. It's no secret, I had a crush on her then, probably still do. When I got back from Basic, I went to work for my dad in the butcher shop. He'd send me to pick up lambs at the ranch and I'd see Grace working in the garden or helping Old Cate with the chores. Mostly Grace worked with the sheep, moving them around with her dogs." He stopped to think back.

Hugo looked up at T. Ray seated on the edge of the mayor's antique desk. He was as quiet as he had ever seen his friend. Finally, T. Ray asked gently, "Eli, tell us what happened to Grace."

After a long moment, the mayor told the story. "It was a storm. Came in without much warning off the water. Grace must have been moving the flock with the dogs along the coast trail when one of her border collies went over the edge. That Grace, oh, my," he said quietly. "Damned if she didn't go after that dog. She fell down the cliff all the way to the beach. Broke her neck along the way. Somehow that collie she went to rescue made it back up the cliff dragging its broken hip and found Jack at the beach house. Jack told me he managed to get there in time for Grace to die in his arms." And added, "He wanted me to know that."

Eli stared into his empty mug, searching for one more drop. "Jack could have *climbed* back up the cliff, but he stayed with Grace through the storm until the morning when the Coast Guard could get a chopper to them. Right after the accident, he sent the boy away," the mayor stopped, then went on.

"Nate was only six at the time. Jack sent him to Ireland to live with Grace's family for his schooling. Oh my, did that rile Old Cate. After that, mother and son fought at every turn. Finally, they stopped talking altogether. That's about the time Jack turned to drink for a while. He was never much good at it, drinking, I mean."

There was no mistaking that the man looked a bit lost in the telling. Hugo imagined Eli might have taken a drink or two himself after Grace went over the cliff. It reminded him that he had once felt that way about a girl.

After thanking the mayor, Hugo led T. Ray into the hallway of the splendid City Hall. T. Ray stopped in his tracks. "Sandoval, I think I'm going to hang back and speak with the sheriff when he gets here. I'll meet you at the ranch." T. Ray kept hold of the lead. "Here's what I want you to do—you're going to drive half a mile north of the farmhouse. When you see old barns on both sides of the road, park there and wait for me. I won't be long. And don't wander off!"

The last comment was a little dramatic for T. Ray who, as Hugo had noticed, had pulled out his Dashiell Hammett impersonation. In his opinion, Harrison was too muscular for Hammett, but he was passable where it counted.

As instructed, Hugo parked the BMW on the northern edge of the Dillon ranch and waited for T. Ray. He found it to be a hotspot for cell phones which allowed him to text Sara.

3:22 p.m. / pull recent articles on illegal cannabis grows in Mendocino —HS

3:29 p.m. / look at Jack Dillon's service record + discharge from Marines. 1990. —HS

3:30 p.m. / find anything on Deputy Andy Ruiz, Mendocino County Sheriff—HS

Due west, the headlands above Chicken Cove and the point beyond reminded him of a painting he had seen that morning in a storefront window in town. In the painting, the fog had all but vanished, disappearing beyond the horizon. Looking now at the Pacific, he could see a thick shadow line of the fog scored on the horizon, waiting, while soaring over the empty headlands, a pair of turkey vultures cut through the clear skies. He envied their views of the coastline.

Despite his limited view, he could see through the cypress grove and trace the multiple roofs that capped the three-story Victorian. *She*—the Victorian, not Cate—appeared to be sitting upright but comfortably, like a queen expecting the arrival of her subjects. Grand and elegant as she was in her day, but that day had passed. The house reminded Hugo of the stories he had heard of its aging matriarch, in a word, *imposing*.

The business end of the ranch peeking out from behind the farmhouse also intrigued with its large horse barn and paddock. Silhouettes of outbuildings and the old dairy barn tucked into the hills filled out the profile of the historic ranch nicely. The only building on the ranch out of sight, as far as he knew, was the modern beach cottage. While Hugo was eager to explore, now was not the time.

Working pickups and slick ranch trucks were scattered among the late-season tourists in late model cars passing the ranch on the highway. Out of nowhere, a white SUV sped past Hugo's position heading south. *Sheriff, Mendocino County* was emblazoned in bold green next to a gold badge on the side of the vehicle. He watched as the patrol car's brake lights tapped on as it approached the turn into the ranch, but the SUV didn't turn. Instead, it sped up, passing the congregation of official cars on the headlands, only to disappear out of sight—just as a Navy helicopter approached from the water.

"Can't be," Hugo muttered, thinking back to Sara's text. *"Holy shit!"*

T. Ray pulled up his truck alongside the BMW. "Ride with me, Sandoval," he shouted through the open window. The lookout slid onto the Chevy's torn passenger seat while T. Ray idled the old engine.

"The name on the red tag is A. Ruiz, Deputy Andy Ruiz, right? I just checked with the Sheriff and A. Ruiz pops up on *Jack's accident report*. Ruiz was the first deputy on the scene when Dillon wrapped his pickup around a stout cypress trunk up at Ten Mile in June. *Coincidence?*" He paused to take in his chief's reaction.

Hugo did not look happy.

"Sheriff's trying to track him down right now. It looks like Ruiz took an unauthorized leave yesterday. And get this—Andy Ruiz worked *for Cate Dillon* years before applying to the police academy. Ruiz was her ranch foreman until Jack kicked him to the curb."

"Ruiz drive a mud-caked SUV patrol car with a serious scrape along the passenger's side panel?" Hugo still wondered where the rogue cop was headed when he'd flown by.

"Jeez," said T. Ray, shaking his head, "Okay. We better let the lieutenant up ahead know."

"Harrison, I know Mrs. Dillon is expecting us this afternoon, but first I need you to take a look at the beach cottage and tell me if I have it all wrong. Nate left it open for us while he's helping Ava with the whale."

T. Ray's truck rumbled past the barricade onto the headlands of the ranch toward the cluster of sheriff's vehicles and parked near the Airstream. Across the field, Hugo recognized a familiar figure walking away from the Navy's Sea Hawk helicopter.

It was the woman who had once told him she would never leave him.

19

HUGO LET T. RAY TOUR THE INSIDE of the beach cottage alone while outside on the deck, he struggled with his checklist. The determined inspector made little progress connecting the dots as the image of Carmen escorted from the helicopter by a Navy pilot kept popping into his head. That image went so far as to spoil the breathtaking view through the trees of the sparkling Pacific.

"Do you think the kid suspects foul play in his father's death?" T. Ray called Hugo from the kitchen while the forensic investigator photographed each pried-up floorboard and missing threshold in the hand-crafted cottage.

"Possibly."

"Christ, Sandoval what's with all the guns?" T. Ray joined the inspector who was trying to decipher the construction of one of Nate's sculptures still hanging on the wall. Both stood there, staring at the intersections of driftwood and salvaged fish netting. "This isn't about a red tag at all, is it, Sandoval?"

"No, I don't think it is."

"You think this is the same set up as the hotel down in Dogpatch?"

"Yep."

"Let me just make sure."

T. Ray fit a cap close to his head before crawling under the structure for a closer look. He had been a champion wrestler in high school. Looking down the throat of sixty, he still had some good wriggling moves which helped him navigate through the redwood stumps and piers on which the cottage stood.

Hugo paced topside, impatient to hear if T. Ray would confirm his suspicions.

"Sandoval—you were right!" the muffled explorer shouted from beneath the deck. But it was a dog, not Hugo, who barked in response. As T. Ray scooted out from under the cottage, Lobo pounced on him with licks and a four-legged takedown. Not far behind the pup, a woman emerged from the wooded path.

"You were right about what?" asked the impeccably dressed Carmen.

"Is this super-hearing thing a family trait? You're as spooky as your boy here," T. Ray laughed as he brushed off the cobwebs and dry leaves before greeting Hugo's ex with warm kisses on cheeks. As usual, T Ray had to take a step back to steady himself. Every damn time he saw her, it was like it was the first time. "You're looking well, gorgeous!"

Hugo appeared from the ocean side of the cottage just in time to witness T. Ray blush as Carmen rubbed off her lipstick mark on his cheek. "Harrison is just doing a little maintenance inspection for Nate before we go see Ava's whale," he lied to his ex for the second time in as many days.

Carmen reached out for Hugo's hand to pull her up onto the deck. He obliged. "Right, so this has nothing to do with a red tag on this place," she commented with a touch of skepticism. "Ava told me how you rushed up here. That was very good of you, Chief Inspector. With all your duties hanging over you at Otis Street, I'm amazed you could get away."

Hugo pretended not to hear her and returned to his inspection of the view side of the cottage.

"Give it up, Hugo," said Carmen. "You knew the spot Ava was

in at Pier 50 yesterday morning. I'm just curious, mind you—why so evasive? I distinctly recall you saying that you had not spoken with our daughter in quite some time—and yet, here you are!" Her accent did not cover the sting.

"Yes, here I am, as are you. To be clear, *technically*, I had not spoken with Ava."

"Technically?"

"Exactly." Hugo continued, on the defensive. "Ava and I had exchanged a few text messages back and forth; fragments to be more precise. She was out of range, and since I didn't have all the facts—" He threw up his hands as if he were making a point. "Look Carmen, it would have been rude to worry you."

"So, you were thinking of *me* when you lied to me." She walked toward the back of the deck.

"And it looks like you lied to me. Why are you here?" he called after her.

Carmen turned on an expensive heel and came close enough to whisper. "Hugo, don't you see that in the midst of all this chaos and everything that is piled on her plate right now, our sweet girl is trying in her own way to bring us together?"

"That's absurd." Hugo forced a laugh at the thought. "You're suggesting that Ava rented a Navy helicopter to fly you up here so we could go on a date?"

"Well, she did insist the Academy bring me up here, although I think the helicopter was just a convenience. The director was dying to see the whale. Look, it doesn't matter," Carmen said backpedaling a bit, "All I'm suggesting is—"

"Ava's not a kid anymore, Carmen." Hugo cut her off.

"Whoa, slow her down, kids," interrupted T. Ray. "Carmen, you'll be staying with us, I hope? I'm sure you have already spoken with Daisy, who is—." T. Ray looked around as if he had forgotten her. "Um, where is my wife, by the way?"

"Daisy is on the beach with Ava. She's been put in charge of the volunteers," Carmen informed T. Ray. Suddenly she shouted, "No! Lobo, Lobo, come back here!"

The dog was on a flat-out run towards the cliff at Chicken Point with the three of them in pursuit. "Please don't let it be a skunk," she huffed, jogging along in her heels. But both Hugo and T. Ray were worried that Lobo might be chasing the same phantom siren call—which had lured Grace's collie over the edge. Before they could catch him, Lobo stopped as quickly as he had taken off, and started howling from the middle of an old ranch road.

Breathless, T. Ray, Hugo and Carmen met up with the possessed pup not twenty feet from the cliff's edge.

"Lobo, you daft mutt, what has got into you? I better take him back to his mum," said Carmen. As she snapped the leash on his collar, she saw a flood of relief on Hugo's face. "It looks like you've had a fright, darling. Are you alright?" Carmen's concern went unanswered as Hugo backed away from the cliffs and squatted to catch his breath. "I forgot, the vertigo."

T. Ray shrugged. "He's fine, Carmen. I'm sure we'll figure it all out tonight at the pub over a couple of pints."

After Carmen was out of sight, and more importantly, out of hearing range, Hugo asked, "Harrison, what do you really know about Nate Dillon?"

"Not much. The buzz about town is he's a good kid with a touch of the delusional, probably runs in the family. What I do know is that a blue-collar town like this one doesn't often take to conceptual artists, even if it's one of their own."

T. Ray picked up on Lobo's last position and followed an old roadbed towards the cove, with his phone snapping photographs of fresh tire tracks on the overgrown grasses and sandy soil.

"Sandoval, these tracks are from a heavy-duty quad, beefy, not your typical ranch model." T. Ray crouched near the spot where Lobo had howled, just shy of land's end.

Hugo surmised, "Jack Dillon probably used this road for a

supply route when he was building his beach cottage. Look. The tracks head to the tunnel; it looks like a shortcut to the farmhouse and barns. His wife might have used it to bring feed to her sheep. When was all that going on, twenty years ago?"

"Yes, but these tracks are fresh. Who made these and why do they go past the cottage towards the Cove?"

"Dunno. Maybe Nate has been hauling his salvage up from the beach?"

"Does he even own a quad?"

"This morning he used a wheelbarrow to take a load back to his truck. We should ask him tonight how he gets around the ranch."

"Yeah, and then ask him about this," T. Ray held a dried-out cannabis seedling. "I found little groups of these plants below some of the gaps in the floor. All about two inches long. It was if they fell through. But what are they doing here?

"I smelled pot in the cottage, but I thought it was Nate being an artist," added Hugo. "Let's hold off asking Nate about the pot until we know more. This morning, he was in the dark about his father's guns. I'm not sure how much he knows about his cottage—or about his father's life while he was away. Let's split up, Harrison. I'll follow the tracks; you head to the Cove. Let's see what we find—although I'm not sure what we're looking for."

"Okay, Chief. And, *Chief*, when you check the outbuildings for the quad, don't just stare at the architecture," said T. Ray.

Although the investigator joked, Hugo could see that something else was bothering T. Ray. Hugo made a note to ask him about it at the pub later after he spoke with Nate. More importantly, what's the real reason Carmen was on the North Coast?

And where the hell was Ruiz going at ninety miles an hour?

20

T. RAY FOLLOWED THE QUAD TRACKS along the cliffs until they ended in a fresh puddle of oil at the edge over the cove. He figured the leaking quad had been parked at that spot for a while.

What was the quad's driver looking for, he wondered? Outside the jagged rocks that configured Chicken Cove, the sea stretched to the horizon and back again. Was it just the view or had the driver been looking for something in the cove below? Whales, perhaps?

As T. Ray surveyed the cove, he found the scene below tilted to the surreal, a still life with the splashes of oranges and reds from living sea stars clinging to the rocks encircling the massive body of the blue whale cradled in the tidepools. But for T. Ray, what knocked him for a loop was the stranded white calf which appeared to be sleeping peacefully on the sand beyond the jagged rock wall that separated mother from newborn.

Only when he worked his way down the cliff face did the scale of the magnificent blue whale come into focus. Daring a perilous shortcut, T. Ray landed near the beach where Daisy, suited up with slicker, rubber gloves and boots, greeted him with a single clothes pin.

T. Ray politely declined the improvised device. "You know I can't smell anymore, darlin'. Tell me, what's Carmen doing here, Daze?"

"The Academy brought her up here to negotiate a deal for the blubber, if you can imagine," Daisy laughed, keeping her eye on the crew. "Look at Ava. She certainly knows her way around a whale. Oh, Ray, don't miss this shot!"

T. Ray brought out his iPhone 4 and started to document the scene. The couple cheered as Ava slid off the back of the mother blue to the beach to join them. T. Ray showed Daisy and Ava the photos in his phone, including the cliff-views of the volunteers flaying away at the whale.

Close in, he observed that the more experienced urchin divers used Yurok hand-forged flensing tools. One style of knife mimicked a hockey stick while another reminded T. Ray of a shovel with a hammerhead blade.

"Dr. Sandoval. We need you at the calf," said a baby-faced, towheaded grad student from Humboldt State's necropsy team. Daisy struck out after the kid, climbing over the hard rocky spine that separated beach from tidepool.

"Before you go, Ava," T. Ray stopped her. "What made those marks on her tail?" They both watched Nate at that moment, standing in water and guts, awkwardly measure the shallow cuts near the whale's fluke.

"I was going to ask you. Nate thinks those are rope burns, but that doesn't make any sense." When the puzzled Ava looked up at him, she relaxed.

"You know you could have called me right away," he chided. "I would have come, any hour of the night."

Ava smiled. "I'm so glad you're here, Uncle T—you *and* my father, of course."

"So, what's up with this guy?" T. Ray asked as they watched Nate struggle to peel off his slicker that was clinging to his wet suit underneath.

"I don't know yet." she shook her head. "I can tell you he's a piece of work. Sweet as pie, but he has secrets."

Scaling the rocks to the far beach, Ava caught up to the other side of the sad story, where the newborn whale lay in repose. While Daisy worked with the team to secure the beach from the public, Ava joined her mother, who had tears running down her cheeks.

"Darling, this is breaking my heart." said Carmen.

Ava put her arm around her mother. "I know, it's awful. What a loss."

"Remember, not a word to Dad about, well, you know."

"You mean, don't tell Dad I didn't call him first? Or don't tell Dad it was your idea to call him all along?" Ava teased. "Got it, Mom."

Back at the blue's carcass, the crew tried to cajole T. Ray into cutting away the blubber, but he politely declined. The forensic investigator hugged the cliff to stay dry. While he worked his way towards Nate, T. Ray grabbed a rusted ring anchored in a boulder; the ring was bigger than his fist.

The observant Nate explained. "The metal rings are all over these rocks. They were drilled in to moor ships while lumber was loaded to their decks from the mill above."

"How exactly did that work?" T. Ray wondered, standing at the base of the steep, weeping cliff walls.

Nate finished peeling off his wetsuit and laid it out to dry on the rock wall next to his sack of beach finds.

"Chicken Cove is one of the doghole ports," he told T. Ray while he pulled on his hoodie. "Tiny inlets barely wide enough for a dog to turn around in, much less a ship. Dozens of doghole ports were scattered up and down this coast back in the 1800s when the most efficient way to get the lumber from sawmills to market was by ship. Each one was a little different. This cove used a chute from the cliff top right about where Ava's Airstream sits. The men would slide the lumber down the chute right onto the ship. But the trick was, the ship had to hold fast; that's what the rings are for. Or so my dad told me."

T. Ray would pass this on later; Hugo would love this story.

"My grandfather, Big J.D—he and his brother purchased the

ranch from the original lumber baron who also built the farmhouse back in the 1880s. Rogers James was his name, I think. It was his mill's lumber that shipped from this port. But that was all long gone by the time my family arrived. Gran will know more. I can show you and the chief photos up at the house if you're interested."

T. Ray smiled at Nate picking up Hugo's nickname. "Ava told me you think these marks on the tail were made by ropes." T. Ray snapped a few more photos at sea level just as the returning tide gently lifted the fluke.

"Yes, sir, I do." Nate dug through his canvas sack of the day's bounty until he came up with what he was looking for and presented T. Ray with a fisherman's knife. "Found it on the wall over there next to the blue. It's a rigging knife. Fishermen call that cone-shaped blade a marlinspike; it's used for—"

"—releasing knots in ropes," finished T. Ray. He balanced the weight of the knife with its custom bamboo handle against what started to taste like anger. "Nate, I'm going to borrow this. And if it's no trouble, tell the inspector that I'll meet him at the pub."

"Where can I find him?" Nate shouted after him, but by then T. Ray had climbed up the roped-off cliff to his truck.

Though he was an experienced poker player, T. Ray could not begin to calculate the odds of the convergence of a blue whale, a red tag, his niece, her new beau, and the meaning of whatever this was in his pocket all on a remote doghole port on the Mendocino Coast.

As the old Chevy rumbled along to Noyo Harbor, its driver hoped the beach artist's *find* would level out the odds.

21

THE QUAD'S TRACKS LED HUGO AWAY from the cliff, across the headlands and into the gulch where he saw tire treads mixed with muddy hoof prints climbing the embankment. There was no doubt in Hugo's mind; the quad tracks would lead him directly to the south end of the Dillon Ranch where three weathered outbuildings large enough to house the quad remained standing. Bowing to T. Ray's request, Hugo made a note to explore them later. It was nearly 4 pm; Cate Dillon should be on her constitutional.

Hugo caught up with Nate's gran at the weather station. The Pacific sun had taken on a ring of gray mist by the time the matriarch closed the door on the instruments. She could hear Hugo approach as he thrashed a path through the dry grass.

"My grandson told me you might be by, Inspector," Cate said warmly, her Scottish burr still charming after a long life in America. "Walk with me?" There was little question in her invitation. She retrieved her walking stick from its lean against the simple wooden weather box.

"It's a true Stevenson Box, I see," said Hugo, although he was less interested in the weather station than he was with its keeper.

Cate easily parted the waist-high brush of the chaparral to lead her guest on the path back to the farmhouse. "Ah, are you familiar with weather stations?" she said, turning around to face him.

"Well, only from history books; I've never actually seen one in use. Not much need for them in the City. You see, on any given day, the weather in San Francisco hits 60 degrees and the fog comes and goes. That's about it." Hugo smiled.

After they walked on a bit, she found her stride on the narrow footpath, conquering tangles of roots and rousting butterflies in her path.

"I'm sure you are aware that the inventor of your weather box was the father of Robert Louis Stevenson."

"Aye. You must know the father built lighthouses, then? Clever fellow, but his son, now there's the gold."

"Even though Stevenson only lived a year or so in San Francisco, we like to claim him as our own." Hugo kept up the pace.

"No shame in that. It would be foolish not to claim him. A wonderful writer. He was a Scot, you know; born in Edinburgh, as was I." She stopped for a breath at an old fencepost and gazed out to sea. Out of the blue, she recited Stevenson,

When I was down beside the sea,
A wooden spade they gave to me
To dig the sandy shore.
My holes were empty like a cup,
In every hole the sea came up
Till it could come no more.

And then she laughed like a young girl, "Listen to me!" With a flourish, Cate held onto her boldly flowered shirt with a high starched collar and scarf at the neck. She had worn soft goatskin garden gloves with the fingertips cut away. With her sleeve pulled back, Hugo noticed the same tattoo, *Gertrude*, he had seen on the inside wrist of the waitress at the Blue Crab Shack.

"Yer San Francisco, never did I return to her after I landed from Scotland. When the war was over there was no time, really, besides what did I need? Everything I ever wanted was here. The ranch was pure heaven when I married J.D. It was a good life. Don't get me wrong, Inspector, farming is hard work, but to know the ranch fed a large part of this coast through difficult times, there's the reward." Hugo felt she was holding back as if a passing thought had put her on the defensive.

As they walked on, the conversation shifted. Cate stopped a few times on the path to identify the last of the season's wildflowers before they entered the concrete tunnel which had been burrowed under the highway. The bright yellow of the gumweed, wallflowers and asters clustered along the path were a stark contrast to the barren passage. Once inside the tunnel, the intermittent roar of traffic overhead halted their conversation. Hugo could see that the rumble from above stiffened her back a bit, as if ironing out the gentle stoop of age. Once clear of the dimness, they walked side by side toward the farmhouse.

Perhaps it had been the uneven ground on the path from the Stevenson Box, but it wasn't until they were in the clear that Hugo noticed he was barely her height. A tall woman for her years, Cate reminded him of the canes of the wild chicory stems she had pointed out along the trail; she was very much like that herb's pale blue flower. More than the color, it was that her eyes *danced.* At least that was what he saw that first meeting.

The old woman signaled to an iron bench near the front steps. Sitting, Cate seemed much smaller. To Hugo's surprise, she was eager to talk.

"Nathanial told me you might help the red tag business go away."

"Anything you could tell me about the ranch might help."

"Well, J.D. closed the dairy when Jack enlisted in the Navy in '89. We kept the cattle and sheep going with the help of a foreman. Eventually we could only afford to keep one man on. It was a few rough years; almost broke us, but we survived. We farmed everything that would sell. Jack was getting ready to plant hops when he—*left us* this past summer." Cate paused to take in the man next to her. She noted his sturdy but light build and did she see a touch of gray in the thick crop of hair? All in all, the matriarch was satisfied with what she saw—his hat in his lap, the solace in his eyes.

"I warned him," She lowered her head.

Hugo waited

"I don't take you for a farmer, Inspector, so I'll explain." Hugo shook his head and smiled. "The hops plant is unusual. It needs sun this ranch doesn't have. Too much fog but Jack thought it could be done. I remember the day he came to me and said he found an open meadow in the forest parcel that was perfect for hops. Honestly, it had been years since I walked into that meadow. It's quite a hike you see, but I know it; I know every inch of the auld ranch," she smiled catching herself. "Look at me going on."

"Tell me more about your boy," Hugo coaxed.

"He wanted to build a brewery, right here on the coast. He built that cottage and fine it is, but my son had no idea how to get a brewery going in the dairy barn and never a thought as to how to plant hops. Jack was born stubborn like his father. Maybe he believed that making beer would be a penance for his years of drinking. *Microbreweries are big business, Ma,* he would say, *a good fit for a father and son.* He was building the brewery to bring Nathaniel home and bring the ranch back to life."

"Mrs. Dillon, can you tell me anything about the whale?"

"Other than it's a nuisance, you mean? I am ninety-two, Inspector. What would an old woman know? I take care of the weather box and the kitchen garden out back, but that's my limit these days, I'm afraid."

Hugo was skeptical of Cate Dillon's self-portrait of a useless old lady. The *forever the Scottish lass, all 120 pounds of her* image might sell on the open market, but he could see she was anything but. Proud, determined, defiant and why not? Despite confiding in him about her son Jack, Hugo sensed she was holding back.

"I'm getting tired now but please come back, Inspector. I'd like to hear more about this whale." With Hugo's hand, and her cane, Cate rose to her feet. She allowed him to escort her to the front porch but no further. "I'll ask my grandson to bring your daughter along; I would like to meet her. Five o'clock is early for Scottish tea, but I promise, you won't go away hungry."

"Unnecessary but most kind. We'll look forward to it."

Turning her back she added, "My Nathanial told me you were a fan of architecture. Have a walk around, the ranch is open to you. Many of the barns date back to the 1800s. One wall of the milking barn is part adobe. The curator at the historical museum believes it was constructed in the late 1600s. Imagine." And with that, she closed the door to the great house.

Hugo took a minute to appreciate the view from the porch landing with the deep blue of the Pacific peeking through the cypress. It was extremely beautiful, but also disturbing. It was not difficult for him to imagine the highway roadbed had isolated, even severed the farmhouse from the sea.

As he heard the roar of the waves breaking offshore, Hugo thought about laughter. He knew laughter to be more than a simple release of emotion or even a response, often, it was profoundly revealing. Walking away from the farmhouse he recalled Cate's laughter after she recited the poem on their walk. Intimate and trusting, her laughter had erased the forty years between them. He resisted looking back over his shoulder, but it was difficult. Hugo was smitten—but he couldn't shake the feeling that Cate Dillon was leading him down the garden path, right past the red-tagged cottage to the cliffs above Chicken Cove.

22

STARING DOWN THE FURY OF THE PACIFIC was a huge leap for the reluctant exile from the city—and not just in a physical sense. Hugo's contact with the ocean before his daughter's cry for help had been limited to summer excursions to Ocean Beach with Carmen and Ava. Growing up in North Beach, the mysteries of Chinatown loomed only a block away for the young Hugo, and dangerously so. Whatever had been sticking out of the ice mounds in the window of Henry Fong's seafood market on Jackson Street told tales of a mythical saltwater world, far beyond the sands of Ocean Beach. The snapper, black bass, stripers, squid, eel, all neatly lined up for sidewalk viewing were disturbing enough—until his mother would drag him inside Fong's, the boy faced a nightmare of bubbling tanks packed with live Dungeness crabs fighting for air, bus tubs of dead redfish with bulging eyeballs, and twitching lobsters packed tighter than the 30 Stockton bus. As a result, Hugo had grown up thinking the ocean was mighty crowded.

Hugo was born to a city sculpted by its geography. He appreciated the symphonic arrangement of the famous San Francisco hills lovingly captured on three sides by ocean and bay. It was those hills and the saddles between that shaped neighborhoods and nurtured diverse cultures. Raised above a Basque restaurant on the border of North Beach and Chinatown, Hugo's world was a bottomless cup of internal refugees of which he was one.

Even at a young age, he recognized that the complexity of economic and ethnic elements around him—languages, traditions, food, music—were all part of the brew. He was hooked early on and explored as if he were ordained by Marco Polo himself. Hugo continued to roam the 49 square mile peninsula as an adult. To ground his thoughts, the building inspector and Venetian's acolyte, often sought out his favorite perches to restore his ballast and clarity with his city.

Whether pedaling his Gitane or on foot, Hugo could reach his favorite perches throughout the City, beginning with Klockar's on Folsom Street, where, when standing next to 82-year-old blacksmith Tony Rosellini, he could observe a cross-section of the downtown rise through the open shop doors, a view that revealed a constant morphosis of the skyline accented with colorful comments from Tony's eclectic posse; and at nearby Red's where, randomly seated at the counter of the waterfront dive, the city boy could hold court at water's edge while people-watching over a ham sandwich. In Washington Square Park, Hugo always found his footing and Rocco, his patron. Their park bench provided courtside seats to a ground game of cultures living in harmony; and up a circular staircase to the top of Fort Point, where the intimidating view from the roof beneath the arch of the russet golden bridge challenged his acrophobia. Finally, returning home to the rooftop of JM's Edwardian flat, by far the most reflective, intimate view and one which required of the explorer little or no advance planning; a familiar perch where Hugo could find solace in knowing the view had changed little in his lifetime.

As he approached the rocky spine of Chicken Cove, Hugo thought how, as the son of immigrants whose lives had been cut short, he had worked hard to nurture a legacy he could pass on to his daughter. It was crazy but he had to wonder if he had really told her how proud he was of her, of her independence, of her heart. Here she was before him, completely at home, knee-deep in swirling tidepools in the lingering autumn of 2011; as good a time as any to show his faith in her.

Ava looked up from the messy necropsy on the blue to watch her father climb to a new perch above the beach. *What was he thinking?* Although no more than maybe two stories above sea level, the rocky spine was beyond his limit. A shot of fear ran through her. It made her think back to the time when he took the hand of a timid seven-year-old, and together they climbed out a stubborn casement window onto a balcony of her elementary school. "Courage," her father told her that day.

Now, covered up to her chest in the cetacean's blood and guts, Ava remembered how the two of them looked down on the school grounds and watched her schoolmates line up for the buses or walk home hand in hand. They could see some stayed behind on the playground where a basketball would appear or a book, or a half-eaten sandwich. She could see over the rooftops of the City, even through the cables of the Golden Gate Bridge to the shimmering ocean beyond.

And so, while standing inside the belly of the whale, Ava knew exactly what her father was doing 20 feet above her, where he was precariously but tenderly balanced on the rocks.

"*Courage*," Ava exhaled.

With a solid base in California geology, Hugo knew he was climbing on the leading edge of an active plate. Securing his Borsalino, he worked his way between the tidepool and the open beach towards the point. Fear of drowning was dwarfed by the desire to see how the blue could have possibly navigated the old doghole port, twice. As he made his way along the spine, he imagined ships tying up to the rocks, the chutes sending lumber down from the flat headlands. If a ship could sail through the entrance to Chicken Cove, why not a whale?

Careful to avoid spikey urchins, flowery anemones, and piano key clusters of goose barnacles in the pits and puddles of the tidepools, Hugo pressed on. Near the point he startled a black oystercatcher with fetching orange bill and feet. The shorebird protested the intrusion with a series of sharp cries and *weeers,* but Hugo remained steady. The thunderous roar of the ocean greeted him at the highest viewpoint, wrapping him in a seductively rich sea mist where Hugo became one with the cove and part of its story as he balanced on the pinnacle. The exhilaration of the climb was only muted by the drama of the scenes below. On one side of the rocky spine, the deconstructed ninty-foot-long blue whale remained wedged in the crook of the tidepools, while on the other side, her newborn calf rested on soft sands.

From his new perch, Hugo observed the wave action rushing through the isthmus to Chicken Cove. What was the secret to entering this narrow passage so vehemently defended by rocks above and below the surface? In the last notes of daylight, he tried to imagine the final ride of the whale and her calf. There was no question in his mind, it was a one in a million shot.

Resting in the tidepools, the mother whale's skin that remained intact showed the impact of the pinball-like ride, but her calf was practically unmarked as it lay peacefully on the crescent-shaped beach. How had the newborn become stranded on the far side of the rocks without getting banged up? Hugo dismissed Ava's theory that, while the blue had most likely given birth in the Cove, the tides alone were responsible for separating mother and calf. From his perch, Hugo watched wave after wave confirming what he suspected. The cetologist's theory just didn't hold water; the sea was not to blame.

The October tides were seasonally low, but even so Hugo was in danger of stranding himself. For a moment he was frozen with fear, but he remembered how his therapist taught him to breathe. Ava waved with both arms for him to return to shore but before he scrambled off the rocks, he took a long look at his daughter. Below him Ava stood knee-deep in fifty-degree tidepools with one reassuring hand on the whale as her crew secured her for the night. Hugo snapped photos to send to Sara back at Otis Street.

On the beach, Hugo's Borsalino no longer smelled of the estuarine waters of the San Francisco Bay; the fedora had taken on the salty sea spray of the Pacific. When his daughter playfully took it from his head and placed it on her own, Hugo grimaced as his girl, suited in flesh-splattered hip waders, fitted the Borsalino to her head with her bright blue elbow length whale-speckled gloves.

"What's next?" Hugo asked his fearless daughter. The image of the 10-year-old Ava's triumphant face after her solo row across Stow Lake matched the radiance of the woman's face before him.

"Dinner, I hope. Dad, what an amazing day." Ava was tired but excited.

"I'm so proud of you," her dad confessed.

She gratefully took it in but then considered what was next indeed. "The vet from the marine lab opened up the major organs and collected samples all afternoon; that's done. And I know Daisy and her volunteers are hoping to preserve the bones for the town, but we still have about 80 tons of blubber to cut away; it's an enormous task. Thank goodness members of the Yurok tribe arrived with special knives to speed things up."

"So why the long face, baby?"

"I'm not sure we have enough time. Progress is slow and we still haven't figured out how to get sections of the blue up the cliff; it's too dangerous by hand." Ava couldn't hide the angst in her voice. "In a week the high tides return. When they do, we'll lose her."

23

The Lost Inn and Pub was comfortable. Back in his room, Hugo again admired the details, especially the original corner sink. He guessed it to be 1910 vintage with nickel handles and spout, matching the shower fixtures he had just used down the hall.

It had been a scant hour since the building inspector relinquished his perch at the Cove. He was relieved that he didn't embarrass himself in front of Ava. Before tucking his shirt into the complimentary garment bag, he held it to his face for one final taste of the salt spray. The Borsalino was another matter. Lightly infused with rotting whale, the fedora required a damp wash cloth and rubdown.

Although strangely invigorated by his afternoon adventure to the sea, he had not forgotten why he was on the coast. It was time to rest and reflect on the day's events. When he closed his eyes, Hugo combed Chicken Cove as if it were any other structure in the City, recreating the flow of the current in his head, the break of the waves on the rocks, and the relentless tide filling and draining the small inlet.

The city boy in him was relieved to see that his No. 1 had packed not one, not two, but three near-identical Irish linen shirts. He suspected that Sara had called Kim at Tower Laundry to reroute the delivery of his weekly sky-blue-paper-wrapped laundry to

Otis Street. While Hugo had come to expect that level of detail in a normal run of activities at the department, this was over the top. Hugo had long recognized his assistant's invaluable skills. But this deserved an extra thank you. He made a mental note to bring back a bottle of Lost Coast wine to Sara as a token of his gratitude.

With that thought in mind, Hugo knotted, then loosened his vintage tie, before heading down the steps to the pub to meet the other essential part of his team, T. Ray.

The Lost Pub was filling up. Locals, spectators, and volunteers were trading stories about the whales. Leaning back on the beadboard wall near the entry, Hugo tipped his Borsalino forward, tuned out the din of the pub and closed his eyes to review his infernal checklist. Sadly, it was all in pieces. He needed Harrison; hell, he needed another beer.

Top of the list, the split. He considered the calf. It was too far up on the sand to have made it on its own. Besides, its umbilical cord was still attached suggesting that the 750-pound newborn washed up onto the beach still tethered to his mother or shortly after its birth. On the other side of the rocks, the big blue, all 50 tons of her. Clearly, she had moved to the tidepool side of Chicken Cove leaving her calf behind. After observing Chicken Cove from the rocky spine, it was clear to Hugo that even the most calculating and insidious of tides would have required assistance to relocate a whale that size from her beach landing to the tidepools. That only left *who helped* and *why*?

Ping.

He had messages. Hugo resettled with a fresh pint at the large round in the corner of the pub and scrolled through texts from Sara while he waited for Harrison to show.

4:05 pm PDT - Sea Star heading to port as per protocol after hitting a whale; course - 162.0 degrees, speed 10.1 knots, 72 meters long —SD

4:07 pm PDT - 2 of the 5 whales hit on Pacific Coast in September were blue whales— SD

4:10 pm PDT - Chief, where did you hide the blue bottle? —SD

He was waiting on T. Ray, but trouble showed up first. Carmen's thick, wavy hair had been tossed by the Pacific winds to great effect. Showered and fresh, she appeared, at least to Hugo, to be invigorated rather than to be worn by her arduous day, which had started with a helicopter ride from San Francisco.

"Expecting company?" Carmen looked at the empty seats around the table.

Hugo straightened in his chair and put away his phone. "Harrison is missing in action. You didn't run into him at their house, did you? Daisy mentioned that you're staying with them," he added casually.

"I'm sure he'll be along, Hugo." Carmen's confident tone was unnerving. "He probably got the wires crossed and went back to the house to pick up Daisy."

Exactly at that moment, Ava and Daisy spun through the revolving door. T. Ray was not in sight.

"Look at her. Our girl," she sighed as if twisting the knife. "Ava was a rock star today, Hugo, but you were there, of course, overseeing." Carmen cocked her head at the thought of Hugo on the rocks as she waved over her friend Daisy, who was working the crowd by introducing Ava to new prospective recruits.

"You saw her out there today, it was her show!" Daisy declared as she approached the table. "*Absolutely brilliant, dahling,* as her mother would say." Daisy mimicked Carmen's accent. "Thanks to your Ava, this beautiful creature will be rescued from further tragedy and insult. You know, *mes chers*, I believe the director of the Academy was extremely impressed. *C'est incroyable.*" Daisy always worked in her showy French accent when she wanted to make a point.

Daisy embraced Hugo with a long hug, a short lecture, and kisses on both cheeks. "*Mon Dieu*, Hugo, what *have* you been doing? You're all bones. You will stay with us, no? No means yes, my love." She turned to Carmen. "Sit, sit, sit," Daisy insisted, settling in at the round table next to Carmen.

"That's very sweet, thank you, Daisy, but I have a splendid room upstairs." Hugo was adamant.

"*Quel dommage.*" She frowned for Carmen's effect.

Hugo would be the first to admit he dropped a few pounds which showed on his small frame. All in, he thought he looked pretty good considering he was perpetually restless and had long tired of eating out alone.

The sight of three beautiful women at the corner round in his pub was too much for the proprietor. Fitz showed up bearing complimentary baskets of the house's special fish and chips for the table before leaning into Hugo's ear.

"You know, Inspector, I could use your opinion on the back door closer. Won't take a minute." Fitz didn't take his eyes off Carmen, insisting, "*Now* would be a good time."

The barman led Hugo past the urinals and stalls to where T. Ray was washing up at the token sink. Hugo found him trying to keep his head back without falling over, blood all over his shirt, cuts and bruises on his face and hands.

"What in the hell happened to you?"

"I'll get some ice," Fitz said, leaving them alone.

"Thanks," muttered T. Ray, fighting a spinning head.

"Talk to me, Harrison."

"It's what Ben told me at the gas station. Ben said all he needed to do was to make a single phone call to any one of a half dozen fishing boat captains and they'd go after those sinkers, legal or not."

Hugo nodded, "Right. The submerged logs, yeah, I get it, the fishermen are desperate."

"When I saw what I saw with Nate this afternoon on the beach, well, I just had to find out."

"Find out what? Who did this to you?"

Although the smaller of the two, it was Hugo who usually finished the fights. T. Ray always said it was the Cuban in him.

The flickering fluorescent lighting in the men's room was less than flattering and made T. Ray's blood look like chocolate sauce. The cut over his left eye started to bleed through the makeshift bandage.

"I was inspecting the *Tango II* when they jumped me. I think my head hit a seam in the deck where pins were coming loose. Probably a code violation," T. Ray said,

"I'll let it pass," said Hugo. The pungent smell of a rancid stew wasn't coming from the pub's kitchen but from T. Ray. Hugo smelled fish guts, seagull poop and stale beer.

"Broken winch or not, the two lugs who clocked me had a point, Sandoval. I *was* trespassing."

"Can you identify them?"

"Their voices maybe," T. Ray tried to smile. "They sounded more like characters from a Martin Scorsese movie than presenters at a Ted Talk. When I said I was harmless, I caught the boot. Party over."

Hugo helped T. Ray take off his blood-stained shirt and wash up.

"It's old school, Sandoval. Those deep holes in her tail had to have been made by a gaff, whale-hunter style. Somebody tried to hook her up, somebody who knew what they were doing."

"Like the captain of a fishing boat?"

T. Ray gave a short nod while keeping his head back. "Skip Henshaw told us yesterday he sent his son Moses to Chicken Cove early Thursday morning, just to check. Check what, I wondered? And then he tells us his boy saw the whale, and not only the whale but the gaff marks on the tail, all the way from the cliff. Think about it, Sandoval. Nate's been telling us the beach has been socked in with fog every morning, and just to be sure, I checked with the Coast Guard. To see the whales, much less the marks on the mother's tail, Moses would have had to been down on the beach. There is no way he could have seen anything from the cliffs."

"The kid was on the beach Thursday morning, Harrison, that

fits, but so was Nate," said Hugo. "Nate told us he walked the beach Thursday morning like he does every morning and because the fog was so heavy, he literally bumped into the whale."

T. Ray caught up. "Yeah, in the tidepools exactly where she is now. Nate said he rushed back to call Ava. He never even saw the calf on the beach until later in the day."

"Don't forget, Harrison, your captain friend told us his son saw the calf tucked up against its mother. There is no room in the tidepools for the newborn. Besides, when I inspected the calf today, he hardly had a scratch on him. The calf never left the beach, but his mama certainly did."

"Bastards," uttered the building investigator. "The only way Moses could have seen the mother and calf side by side is if he saw them on the beach Wednesday *before* someone sank gaffs into the blue's tail to tow her out to sea."

"Skip told us he could hear the winch screaming from the phantom ship off Chicken Cove on Wednesday night and then the sound stopped cold—suggesting the winch broke," said Hugo. "Do we believe him?"

T. Ray could see in the mirror that Hugo was almost smiling.

Wincing from bruised ribs, T. Ray pulled a plastic bag out of his pocket and handed it to Hugo. In the bag was the rigger's knife. "The cone-shaped blade is for getting knots untied."

"Where did you get this?"

"Nate found it on a rock near the whale's tail this morning. When he showed it to me, I recognized the mark on the handle. See that funny shaped T, that's the brand for the *Tango II,* Skip's boat.

"Let me get this straight. You went down to the harbor, *alone*, to see if the *Tango*'s winch was broken?"

"Indeed, I did."

"Damnit all, Harrison, why didn't you check with me? or better yet, call the sheriff?" scolded Hugo as he weighed this new development. "Well—was it broken?"

"I didn't get to find out. When I moved toward the back of the boat to check, two guys jumped me. I think I hurt one of them before my lights went out. Tourists on the harbor saw the whole thing and called the Coast Guard," said T. Ray. "Sandoval, why would a fishing boat captain want to tow a whale off the beach?"

"First, we need to know how this captain even knew about the whales at Chicken Cove. Nate was the first to report it when he bumped into the big blue Thursday morning, but from the looks of it, he wasn't the first to know about the stranding."

Fitz returned with a bucket of ice, some thick salve, and a jacket over his arm. The barkeep closed the gash above T. Ray's eye like a cutman ringside. "It probably needs stitches, Harry. There, that should hold for now. I'm dying to hear this story, but the bar's fillin' up. You fellas better get back to the table, your women are restless—oh, and you have company. Harry, put this jacket on. I run a dignified establishment."

"How did you get here from the harbor anyway?" Hugo asked.

"Fitz. He found me passed out in my truck and dropped me at the loading dock."

"You mean the ADA-accessible entrance," corrected Hugo. Feeling both guilty and angry, Hugo helped T. Ray zip up the Lost Pub's dishwasher's leather jacket. The jacket not only disguised T. Ray's bruised chest but neatly held the ice pack against his ribs.

"How do I look?" T. Ray asked Hugo who could only laugh. "Bastard, you're enjoying this, aren't you? Next time, you take a punch for the team."

"It wouldn't have happened if I had been with you."

"Like the time you were with me when a 300-pound Russian came flying out of her filthy kitchen swinging a broom stick at my head like it was batting practice. Yeah, you were there all right, but you decided to slip onto the fire escape—which, by the way, you had just condemned—while she caught me between the fourth and fifth ribs."

"She thought we were from Immigration," added Hugo, laughing.

"Stop. It hurts," cried T. Ray, trying not to laugh.

When Hugo returned to the table with T. Ray, they found that the mayor had joined them along with the president of the Land Trust, a Mrs. Justine Turner, an elegant Mother Earth-ish type of woman in an alpaca Peruvian poncho and silver earrings. Fitz brought over a pitcher of beer and another of margaritas for the table.

When T. Ray sat down, he signaled his wife to hold her comments, but that didn't stop Carmen from shooting a dagger look at Hugo. Eli noticed the alterations to T. Ray's face, but ever the politician, let it go. When T. Ray reached for Justine's hand, Daisy saw pain flash over her husband's face, but was more concerned why he kept his left hand tucked to his chest.

As it turned out, Mayor Eli Callaghan was a respected board member of the Land Trust, but it was Justine who had negotiated with the Dillons, which is why Eli called her in. He felt Justine could help clarify the situation on the Dillon Ranch. But first he had to convince her that revealing details about a land trust deal that didn't go through was within her discretion, and that the board would support her on that.

Small town, Hugo thought to himself, again.

"We spoke about it six months or so before Jack was killed. It was Jack who turned against moving the ranch into a land trust," said Justine, looking to Eli for approval. He smiled.

Watching their back and forth, Hugo immediately wondered if Justine was sleeping with the mayor; he would ask Harrison later.

"*We*?" he asked.

"Apologies, I'm talking about Cate Dillon and her son, Jack. They both were part of the plan although it was Cate who called us in originally. We talked about what is known as a Reserved Life Estate for the Dillon Ranch."

Carmen explained, "That's when the family lives out their lives on the property."

"Exactly," said Justine. "Originally, Jack had other ideas to bring the ranch back to its glory, but Cate was firm and wanted the Land

Trust to take over."

"And the Land Trust would take it on, even if it wasn't free and clear?" asked Hugo.

"Well, Chief, it's not unusual, but it's complicated," Justine said.

Hugo thought his head was going to explode if he heard that word one more time. He looked over at T. Ray who attempted a response but instead, a flicker of pain passed across his face.

"From the beginning, Cate disclosed her debts; the ranch was in desperate need of cash," Justine confided.

"You understand, that is not unusual on the North Coast to be land-rich and cash-poor," Eli added.

"That is indeed the case," Justine smiled gratefully at Eli. "With Cate's wishes in mind, the Land Trust proposed to divide the ranch into three parts. The first part was to be the farmhouse with its barns. That property would be put into a conservation easement, allowing the Dillons to stay on the land until they die. The second part would be the ranchland and creeks to be sold to the Land Trust. That sale would provide the cash injection Cate needed to clear her debts and then some."

"And the third part is the coast," Hugo concluded.

"Yes, Chief, the coastal lands would be donated for conservation outright. The process takes a while, as you can imagine, but we felt confident we could find the money," said Eli. "I'm sorry I couldn't tell you all this earlier. You understand, I needed to clear this with Justine first."

"The plan sounds solid. What went wrong?" The attorney at the table asked.

"When we started the conversation, both Jack and Cate were on the same page. Each had their reasons to conserve the land and its history and at the same time protect it from development," explained Justine.

"A few months later, out of the blue, Cate called it off. She told us that Jack had a new idea for the ranch and that she was going along with her son," Eli chimed in.

"You mentioned development. Was there a developer coming

after it?" said Daisy, throwing her hat into the ring.

"I only wish I knew. Up here there are always rumors," said Justine. "When I asked about that possibility, Cate told me they had been approached but was quiet about the details."

"The next thing we found out was that the liens on the ranch had been paid off," added Eli.

"When was that?" asked Carmen.

"June of this year," offered Hugo surprising everyone at the table.

"How did you know that, Chief?" Eli was impressed.

"The strange thing was that not two weeks later, Cate called to tell me Jack was back on board with the plan. He had a change of heart, exactly what she called it, but she left it at that," Justine paused to sip her margarita. "Naturally, I was delighted but I was also concerned. Cate sounded worried."

Eli nodded, adding solemnly, "It was only a few days after Cate's call to Justine that Jack was killed in the crash up the highway."

"Are you still working with Cate now that her son is gone?" asked Carmen.

Justine looked worried. "That's the funny thing, she's gone cold on the idea of the Land Trust taking over at all."

"Quite a roller-coaster," Carmen commented.

"Chief, I wanted you to hear the whole story," said Eli looking at Hugo. "Maybe you can make sense of it. Jack just wanted to keep running sheep and cattle out there like his dad and his uncle, but with the native grasses all but gone, it was never going to happen. Hell, he was already bringing in most of their feed at elevated prices. Whatever his plan was, at the end of the day I figured it was personal. Jack just didn't want anyone touching his coast."

Justine summed it up for the table as if she were speaking at the Rotary Club. "Land like the Dillon Ranch just doesn't come available every day. The coastal access to the Cove alone is priceless. I won't lie to you; this is exactly what conservancies are looking for. Even so, and I want you to understand, the Trust does more than preserve land, we preserve legacies. The Dillon family has been a big part of the history of the North Coast for nearly one hundred years and I personally don't wish to see that legacy vanish."

Eli escorted Justine through the revolving doors just as Nate entered the Lost Pub. Hugo watched the two men greet each other noticing a certain awkwardness when the two men stood eye to eye.

By the time the young heir to the Dillon Ranch sat down at the big round, it was the only quiet table in the house. T. Ray was huddled with Daisy explaining his condition, while Carmen and Ava sipped their drinks in silence and tried to ignore Hugo, Borsalino down, who, to outsiders at least, appeared to be sleeping. His ex-wife and daughter knew differently.

Fitz returned to the table with a pint glass for Nate and broke the silence. "This one's for you, Jack!" and hoisted his glass.

"To Jack!"

"I only wish Jack could see the entire town rallying around the Cove; it's a sight to behold." Daisy raised her glass.

Fitz, ever the charmer, squeezed between Carmen and Daisy. "It was a few months after I bought this place, the Dillons came right through those doors to this very table. First it was Grace—my, she was a beauty. Then Cate thundered in with a homemade berry pie for me. All of a sudden, my beautiful doors stopped revolving. I could see through the glass, two exceptionally large men stuck in the turn. Jack was a bear, like his father. It didn't look like either of the Dillon men would make it through without breakage. I thought to myself, my doors are finished—my beloved century-old pub doors from Cork, shattered at the feet of the Dillon clan!"

Ava was enjoying the story. She scooted closer to a quiet Nate, putting her hand on his arm.

"When I brought their steaks to the table, Cate wouldn't let me set 'em down. She said she wanted Jack to make her the exact same size table for her kitchen at the ranch. Instead of a tape measure, Jack used his hands to measure. He bragged his spread was twelve inches across to the penny. Five hands across it were. Not to be overshadowed, Big J.D. laid his own hands on the table and measured. What a sight, nearly half his hand fell off the table on the fifth run."

Everyone laughed at the Irishman's story except for Nate. The boy had arrived at the pub in a reflective mood as far as Hugo could see. Regardless, they egged Nate on until the youngest Dillon spread out his hands, walking them across the table, *six* times. A ten-inch spread was respectable, but it wasn't a Dillon hand.

"Sixty inches?" Nate asked the Pub's owner. Fitz nodded.

T. Ray laughed, "There's your mother in you, son!"

"Bravo. Here's to your mother, Grace," said Eli raising a glass.

As the pub's owner gathered up the empty mugs, he asked Daisy a loaded question, "Now, where might you be putting all those bones, Mrs. Harrison?"

"We're going to bury them where no one can find them, especially you, Fitz. You would sell off that skeleton bone by bone if you could," Daisy laughed. "I can see the gift shop now!" Daisy shouted after him.

"Three hundred fifty-six," announced Ava. Everyone at the table looked at the young cetologist. "That's how many bones in a blue whale, three hundred and fifty-six." Ava smiled at Nate. "And with that, it's time for me to call it a night."

"I discovered that there are only a handful of blue whale skeletons on display in the entire world. Those three hundred and fifty-six bones could put this town back on the map," the mayor revealed, tipping his mug to Ava, who nodded in agreement.

As they gathered to go, Hugo cornered Nate while Ava said her goodbyes to her mother; he had one more question for him.

"Nate, are you certain it was a winch you heard Wednesday night?" Hugo asked in a hushed voice looking away from the two men at the bar who had been staring at his table since Fitz made the toast to Jack.

"Yes sir. Absolutely certain. My mother's family are fishermen in Rossaveel on the west coast of Ireland. I lived in their house near the harbor for ten years; I know the sounds of a fishing boat's gears in Gaeltacht and English," said Nate defensively.

"It wasn't an accusation."

"No, of course not, forgive me." Nate seemed upset. "I just can't get that night out of my head. I thought at the time it was odd, a boat fishing inside the marine reserve and inside Chicken Cove, no less. I mean, why would anyone risk it?"

"I've been wondering the same thing."

24

Once Nate and Ava left the pub for the Airstream, it was open season in the bar, with drinks and food flowing to the corner round. Although Hugo wanted to keep the investigation low-key, the alcohol energized his team—even the mayor joined Daisy and Carmen in pressing T. Ray for details of the investigator's misadventure to the *Tango II*. Hugo's mind was elsewhere and leaned back for a *think* inserting Jack's dance with the Land Trust into his list.

Who had paid off the Dillon Ranch debts?

T. Ray's question brought the inspector back to the table.

"What if Nate wasn't at the beach cottage? He might have heard the winch from the farmhouse," suggested T. Ray, holding his cold pint to the side of his head.

"No, the beach cottage is more likely—besides, why would he lie?" Hugo leaned over the table towards T. Ray. "Something is bothering Nate, but I didn't want to push too hard. The kid insists he heard a fishing boat just outside the Cove, but I have to wonder if he *saw* anything that night, or for that matter, what did he see the next morning when he walked the beach and bumped into the whale."

Daisy headed over to the bar where Fitz was busy pulling pints.

Carmen realized that there was more to Nate and the whale than maybe Ava had bargained for. Leaning toward Hugo, she casually cupped her hand to his ear. "What do you think of our baby girl in the middle of all this? Should we be concerned?"

"First, we don't know what *this* is yet. Nate's a good lad; he'll keep an eye on her," Hugo reassured his ex, but he had to admit he wasn't as confident as he sounded.

"Not to worry, Carmen, the sheriff left two deputies out at the Cove for the night," seconded T. Ray.

T. Ray's comment failed to put Carmen at ease. She considered his bruised face and battered ribs and longed for that "ride into the wind, swords at the ready" feeling he and Hugo projected. But what if this time they were in over their heads? Of course, Hugo adored their daughter, but Carmen knew Hugo could easily be distracted by the chase. It was an old argument between them: What comes first—family or job?

Ever since they met, she had admired Hugo's ability to sort out the cases crossing his desk at Otis Street, but took exception when he brought home his work and pushed his family aside. While Carmen had encouraged Ava to call her father about the red tag, she did not expect the complications that were presenting themselves. The North Coast was far from Hugo's comfort zone, which was exactly where she had wanted him. She had wanted Hugo to be reunited with Ava, but now she wasn't so sure. The chase was proving to be more than just exciting, and Carmen needed Hugo to focus on Ava.

"Well, Inspector Sandoval, what should we do next? Clearly you think that everything is just right, that Nate and two deputies are all that's needed," Carmen shot at Hugo with a hint of sarcasm.

Hugo looked straight at Carmen. To his surprise, he had forgotten all about whales and beach cottages or whether Ava and Nate were shagging back at the Airstream. No, at that moment, he was thinking about what Fitz had quipped earlier about his ex-wife. Carmen was most definitely a *looker*.

Hugo finished his pint, leaving Carmen hanging. The boy from the streets of San Francisco had always thought the sophisticated Brit was too classy for a humble civil servant. Perhaps he was right, but in all the noise and chatter of the bar, Carmen looked at home. Here she was, completely at ease in a raucous joint on the North Coast that boasted a back-door entrance past a urinal. Carmen was exactly like her short crop of thick auburn hair, unapologetic and breathlessly tossed. How was it she looked as young as the day he met her? Time had spun backwards and, if he was not mistaken, the seacoast had given her cheeks a rose.

Suddenly, despite the din of the pub, it got incredibly quiet between them.

Breaking the silence, Hugo asked, "Why are you here, Carmen?"

"Ava called me about the whale, of course. She needed her mother to figure out what to do with all the blubber. It's a legal nightmare, as you can imagine."

"That's a relief. You'll straighten it out. So why am I here?"

"You know why—the red tag, but it's no longer about a simple building violation, is it, Hugo? You have a real puzzle on your hands, darling." She leaned in close, taunting.

She was too much. Hugo pushed his chair back from the table. He needed to think.

When Daisy returned to the table, T. Ray wrapped his good arm around her shoulders with some difficulty.

"So where do we start? Come on, Chief, give us your list," goosed Daisy. "I know you've got one in that funny head of yours."

Eli returned from the other side of the pub to rejoin the conversation. "Chief, I'd like to help if I can."

Hugo beckoned him to sit down again and looked over his confidants. Before him was a twist on the old joke: *A mayor, an inspector, an activist and an attorney walk into a bar. The building inspector says—*

"All right, but this stays at the table," Hugo insisted, hunching forward over the 60 inches of ring-stained oak. His conspirators nodded.

"First, the reason I was called up here," he said, looking accusingly at Carmen. "A red tag on the beach cottage."

Bloody hell, he knows I set him up. Carmen tried to look away. Daisy giggled.

"Let's go back to Wednesday evening when Nate Dillon discovers the red tag tacked to his front door. The mayor has confirmed there's no official record of a red tag issued on the Dillon Ranch, either in the sheriff's office or in City Hall. And we know the signature on the tag is Deputy Andy Ruiz.

"Nate says he uses the cottage as his art studio, and it looks like it. The interior of the cottage and decks are full of his salvage sculptures and pieces he drags up from the beach. Late Wednesday night, Nate hears squealing from the cove. He recognizes the sound. He insists it was made by the winch on a fishing boat. He has assured me, just now, that he is *certain* of that fact. The fog was thick that night and the cove was socked in, but Nate is ready to swear the boat was *inside* Chicken Cove. I believe he has more about that night to tell us, but Nate isn't spilling."

Carmen shifted uncomfortably in her chair.

"At breakfast this morning, Nate handed me the red tag. The condition of the tag indicates it was posted in a heavy fog with the moisture blurring most of the hand-written details."

"Has anyone spoken with this Ruiz?" asked Daisy.

Eli responded, "The sheriff is looking for him."

"When I was at the cottage with Nate, he showed me firearms that he had found stashed all over the cottage. Most of the rifles were tucked inside closets but all of them were loaded. Nate discovered the guns when he returned to the ranch in July to take care of Cate after Jack was killed."

"The guns sound like a man preparing for a siege, as if he were defending his castle," said the Brit at the table.

"Tell them about the floorboards, Sandoval," T. Ray leaned in as best he could with his ribs crying.

"Without alerting Nate, I noticed several floorboards had been popped up inside the cottage and thresholds under the doors had been removed, leaving significant air gaps, but why?" asked Hugo.

"Jack was a fine craftsman," Eli said in defense of his old friend.

"I could see the cottage was well-built, a testament to his skills," Hugo agreed, "but these alterations were deliberate and most likely engineered with a purpose."

T. Ray jumped in. "When the Chief showed me the cottage today, the gaps reminded us both of a hotel we inspected years ago. It was in a similar state. Just to be sure, I crawled under the cottage, and I found what I was looking for."

"So that was what you were doing when I caught you? or *Lobo* did! What did you find?" Carmen asked.

"The cottage is built on piers; you can practically see from one side to the other." T. Ray looked to Hugo to finish, his headache kicking in.

"Harrison discovered several piles of dry bark and sticks along with the pieces of the flooring and thresholds removed from the interior of the cottage. He dragged one of the piles out to show me; it had new moss growing on it, so I'm guessing the piles were set in place sometime in the late spring when the cottage was staged," said Hugo.

"Staged for what?" asked Daisy.

"These piles were built as starter fuel, while gaps in the floorboards and thresholds had been opened to make the cottage burn faster."

Daisy, Carmen, and Eli were stunned silent. T. Ray resisted the impulse to rub his head furiously with both hands. It was that very habit, Hugo had pointed out to his friend, long ago, that made him a lousy poker player.

"You mentioned a hotel?" Eli pressed T. Ray.

"I did. In San Francisco. The hotel had similar alterations—thresholds removed, holes cut into ceilings, piles of dry wood tucked into the rafters. It had been an old residence hotel in Dogpatch. The owner intended to collect the insurance after it burned down so he could rebuild it and rent it out for big bucks," said T. Ray.

"This slumlord is in prison, I hope." Eli said, disgusted.

"That he is," said Hugo.

"But why burn down the beach cottage? Was it the insurance angle?" asked Carmen.

"Hard to know at this point." Hugo said. "All we do know is the cottage was staged to burn before Jack died."

Eli took over. "Jack was killed when his truck hit a tree, about ten miles north of here, this past June." He turned to Hugo. "Do you think Jack's accident has something to do with the cottage being staged to burn?"

"Right now, I have no idea why or who planned to burn down the cottage. But I do know that the red tag was never about our whale." Hugo was adamant. "Think about it, the tag was posted Wednesday, *the same day* the blue whale stranded herself in the cove. Nate didn't see it until the next day because he normally enters the cottage from the beach side, not the front door where the tag was posted."

Daisy made a point. "But why post it on the cottage? Why not just serve the farmhouse?"

"I think it was to keep Nate away from the cottage, and away from Chicken Cove—but it didn't work. Nate ended up staying in the cottage Wednesday night which was when he heard the winch," Hugo explained.

"Getting back to your theory that a fishing boat tried to drag the blue out to sea Wednesday night. How does that figure in?" Eli asked.

"It makes no sense. Why remove a fifty-ton whale from a beach in the middle of nowhere?" Carmen, zeroing in on an obvious question.

The table turned quiet. No one spoke, each member of the team deep in thought. Eli played with the condensation on the outside of his beer mug while Daisy slowly rubbed her husband's shoulder to the rhythm of the song on the juke box. Carmen watched Hugo for any sign of life stirring under the Borsalino.

Finally, Hugo broke the silence at the round table. "That's exactly it, Carmen." He looked at her with appreciation. And perhaps—*never mind.*

"Chicken Cove *is* the middle of nowhere. Harrison was a little bit of Indiana Jones this morning. Not only did he identify the starter piles, but he found old cannabis seedlings that had fallen through the cracks of the floorboards. Mayor, you just had the Feds at your place tear out illegal cannabis plants. Tell me, when might that crop be ready to harvest?"

"It should be ready now."

"And how do the growers get their product out of the forests to market?" Hugo asked, making the connection.

"Highways, helicopters," Eli's voice dropped, his jaw set. "I'll be goddamned—and sometimes on the North Coast by boat." Eli pushed back from the table. "Excuse me, I have a call to make," he said, feeling foolish.

Seeing it all come together, Carmen whispered, "You're telling me Chicken Cove is some kind of pick-up zone for an illegal cannabis crop, is that it?"

Daisy chimed in. "At least something makes sense. With the crop ready to harvest, the operation would need the cliffs clear to load the goods to the boat."

"Shh, Daze, we don't want to alert the whole town," shushed T. Ray, who gave the pub a once over to see if anyone was interested in their conversation.

"Is this how you operate at Otis Street?" Carmen marveled.

"Sometimes." T. Ray laughed.

"A deputy sheriff was *told* to post a red tag on the cottage door Wednesday." Carmen dropped into the mix.

"Told by whom?" asked T. Ray.

"Exactly," Carmen said quietly.

"And yes, T. Ray, I saw the fresh tire tracks when Lobo ran out to the point earlier. I presume you believe these were left by our deputy?"

"Andy Ruiz," whispered Daisy, mindful of the crowd nearby.

"Yes, cheers, Daisy," Carmen said, her voice also hushed. "Left by our deputy who drove his quad out to the cottage to nail the red tag to the door—presumably to check on the delivery route." She could see it all coming together.

"That would make it Wednesday when Ruiz saw the whales in the Cove," said Daisy with hushed excitement.

Hugo put his chin on his hand. "You're both on the right track. But who told Ruiz to red-tag the cottage, and who did Ruiz call when he saw the whales washed up at their secluded pick-up point?"

T. Ray jumped in. "It had to be the captain of the fishing boat, Skip. Skip Henshaw of the *Tango II.* He was on payroll to pick up the cannabis crop in Chicken Cove but the whales were a problem. They would draw attention to the cove," he said, rubbing his scalp with one hand.

There was still a piece missing, maybe two pieces. Hugo was worried, and unlike Carmen's suspicions, he never stopped considering Ava's safety, not for one minute. With all eyes on him, Hugo put his cards on the table.

"Ruiz had to get rid of the whale or call off the operation. That takes us to Wednesday night when Skip drives the *Tango II* into the Cove, to hook up the whale and drag her off the beach. So far so good but the blue doesn't cooperate. Instead, she gets caught in the bottleneck of the cove. The tow becomes too much for the fishing boat and the winch breaks. At that point, the whale floats like a cork, getting knocked about on the rocks protecting the cove to be carried to shore again by the sea. Except this time, she lands inside the tidepools, not back on the beach where she left her calf behind," Hugo summed it up.

"You're saying after she was hit by the ship, the blue swam into the Cove and landed on the beach with her calf—and then this fucking fishing boat dragged her all over hell." Carmen was disgusted in trying to imagine the mother's final journey. "*Christ.*"

T. Ray had one more detail for the table. "Thursday morning, the morning after the botched tow, Skip's son Moses climbs down into the Cove in the heavy fog to remove the evidence. He would have found his gear still gaffed to the whale's tail, but Moses made a huge mistake and left behind his favorite rigging knife."

"Ah," Hugo nodded, taking through his list. "Trouble is, that mistake almost got you killed."

Eli returned to the table a bit grim. "The sheriff will be along shortly. He'll want to know everything. What did I miss?"

"We're plugging holes, but a few things don't fit," said Hugo, opening his eyes. "Mayor, maybe you could tell us about Ruiz and the Dillons?"

"Absolutely, Chief. It goes way back. It was the Gulf War and there wasn't a job from here to Eureka, so the three of us enlisted—that's Jack, me, and Andy's big brother Ben."

"Ben Davis from the gas station and Andy Ruiz are brothers?" T. Ray looked over to Hugo, dumbfounded.

"Yeah. I thought you knew," said Eli. "Ben and Andy are half-brothers. Andy's mom is from Mexico; she's Old Ben's second wife. Andy took her last name, claiming he looked more like a Ruiz than a Davis. Anyway, Andy was too young to enlist so he stayed behind to work for Big J.D., who was on his last legs. Andy ran the ranch as foreman until Jack returned from the Navy. With Jack back home, Andy was demoted, you might say. He stayed on the ranch until he left to enroll in the Academy to become a deputy."

Hugo surveyed the room. He could see the town was in a fine mood, laughter along with stories of bravery and triumph spilled over into their pints. The student volunteers from Humboldt State were certainly making a night of it at the Lost Pub. Only one thing bothered him; he had noticed from the far side of the tavern that Fitz had not taken his eyes off Carmen. Despite being served one too many, T. Ray had been watching Fitz, too, and decided to do something about it. Hugo stopped him.

"That's enough for one night, cowboy. Take him home, Daisy, or to the ER, I'm not sure what's best." Hugo said helped T. Ray to his feet. "I'll go with you if you like."

"Thanks, love, I'll manage." Daisy fished around in her husband's pockets for the keys to the Chevy to give to Carmen. "Let yourself in whenever you want. You remember how to get up to the house?"

"I think I'm—." She glanced over at Hugo. "—going to stay here tonight, Daze. Fitz said there was one room left."

"Probably his; watch yourself," Daisy teased.

25

Although it definitely registered, Hugo pretended not to hear Daisy's warning to Carmen about Fitz and helped shovel T. Ray into Daisy's Prius before walking over to City Hall. For twenty minutes he and Eli plied their facts to Sheriff Dan Merten from the rear seat of his patrol car.

When Hugo returned to the pub, Carmen was leaning on the bar, engaged in what appeared to be a heavy conversation with Fitz. Hugo tried to settle his bar tab, but the owner waved him off. He spun back out the doors for a walk, wondering if Carmen would even notice he had left the pub.

The night was chilly, but the wandering building inspector needed to clear his head. Although he had put a serious dent into his infernal checklist, how the blue whale got into the cove in the first place was mind-boggling. His view from the spine dividing the cove had deeply affected him. Outside the noisy pub, Hugo found an eerily quiet town and walked into the intersection outside the Lost Inn for a panoramic view of the main streets.

There wasn't a car moving in town. Hugo heard the pub doors send Carmen out into the night, but he didn't turn to meet her. He waited for her inside the cobblestone detail in the middle of the street.

"Did you know, this part of town was built on an old military base? Nothing left to show for it of course, but still, it's pretty cool," she said.

He looked at her in the streetlight. "What are you doing, trying to impress a guy?" Apparently, she wasn't finished.

"The 1906 earthquake was devastating for the town, many of the buildings collapsed and the ones that remained standing caught fire." Carmen pitched on. "Fitz just told me that."

"Fitz, huh?" Hugo realized that the fog was swirling back into the town. "I take it you're staying at the Inn for the night," he said as they stood awkwardly in the middle of the street.

"Got the last room," said Carmen, leaving Daisy's implication hanging out there. "*And* I have my own wheels for the morning; Daisy left me the keys to the truck. My goodness, T. Ray is a one-man band, I had forgotten."

"He's a good friend—to both of us—and to Ava. Sometimes he gets ahead of himself, like tonight. I should have been with him." Hugo was feeling guilty.

"Hugo, he's an investigator, it's what he *does*," she insisted. "Besides, he can't do what you do. That's why you're a good team."

Maybe it was the way she said his name that reminded him of what he had been missing. "Funny how this fog reminds me of home," said Hugo.

"My goodness. You've only been gone for two days, if that," she laughed.

"I'm serious, can't you taste it? Except up here they've added a little more salt," he said.

"Let's walk," she suggested.

They walked in silence. Hugo saw his checklist hovering in front of him like the blade signs hanging from buildings lining the empty streets; it was difficult to read them in the dark. Just two days, he mused. Who was Jack afraid of? Hugo had been fighting the connection all along. *Could it really be that simple*, he asked himself?

At the corner, the glow from the streetlamps lit up the old Sears

& Roebuck storefront; its neon called to them. They could read the iconic logo etched in gold leaf onto the window glass. As Carmen and Hugo peered in, she announced the features of the new washer and dryer under the banner, "It's Sunny Monday on the Farm."

They walked on. Hugo responded with his own local trivia he had picked up that day. "There's 37 percent unemployment in the county with more than 2,000 foreclosures in the past year alone. The recession is slow to recover up here with the median income at $14,000; that's 20 percent below the national average."

In disbelief, Carmen stopped and stared at him. "That's all you have to say to me, after barely speaking to me the past sixteen months?"

"I thought it was a good opener. I'm out of practice." He wondered about her reaction and waited.

"Theodore thinks you might be a bit dazzled by Nathanial's grandmother. Going for a sure thing?" Carmen teased; Hugo relaxed.

"You know damn well it's Thelonious, not Theodore,"

"How am I to remember what the T stands for? Honestly, Hugo, I've never met a man with so many names."

The pair walked on side by side in easy rhythm, crossing the empty streets as if they were dancing. "He certainly is pugnacious. Just like a Scot," she smiled. "Harrison is Scottish, isn't he? Tweed and whisky and all that?"

"What, Harrison a Scot? Never. He's too soft; no, he's all Aussie. There's a toughness that comes with being a Scot." And then Hugo changed his tone. "She's tough," he acknowledged. "She is tough, but in a beautiful way,"

"Who might that be?" Was Carmen perhaps a little jealous?

"Catelyn McCue Dillon. A Scot with all the trimmings."

Carmen thought he would elaborate but when he didn't, she changed the subject. "Hugo, I'm absolutely starving."

They walked along the dune fence that sanctioned off the old mill property and the coastline from the town. Bleeding through the swirling fog, a neon sign illuminated the disarming pizza den,

Piacci. The bistro was packed tight but, like the sign, it was warm and inviting. The couple found a stool to share until a second one opened up and ordered a pizza.

"I told Ava how you handled Pier 50," Carmen confessed.

"What did I do?"

"Well, maybe it was what you told Sara to do. Absolutely brilliant, Hugo. The archeological dig alone will take months, which might buy just enough time for the owners to get out from under. It's sad, but those women simply cannot continue to fight the Port; they'll never win."

"It was more than buying them some time, Carmen. Take it as a warning to your developers."

"They're just clients," she corrected sheepishly.

"Despite your client's presumptive civic-minded zeal, the waterfront is about legacy. It's exactly like Justine said tonight about the Dillon Ranch. Building a fancy structure out on Pier 50 with swimming pools and all kinds of nonsense while the sea level continues to rise is just foolish and you know it."

Carmen agreed. "Anyway, I wanted you to know Ava said she was immensely proud of you. No doubt it will make all the papers and I know how you *hate* publicity," she poked, knowing Hugo secretly liked his fame.

"Ah, somebody has to stir things up, Carm. Freedom of speech, and you know I can't stop Sara from writing her blog even if I wanted to."

"Do you think she is going to write about the old man you met yesterday? He seemed more than worthy of her blog." Carmen held up her palm. "Stop! Before you answer, I need to know, and be honest with me—what is your fascination with octogenarians of late? Have fifty-somethings completely lost their allure?"

Hugo tried to avoid looking at her as they both huddled over their pizza; he failed.

"I'd say Al Kleinen is more in his nineties, as is Cate," he said thoughtfully. "But it's not the age exactly, it's their *connection*."

"To what?"

Hugo almost let it go, but added, "I've been wondering if the story he told me yesterday was more a premonition than just a story from his early days."

"I'd like to hear it."

Shaking his head, "I doubt if I'd be able to do it justice, I'm afraid. He's a great storyteller."

"The premonition part, then."

Carmen felt Hugo drift away from her. She had experienced *the drift* many times before. At those moments she imagined Hugo to be a fly fisherman casting into a pool, repeatedly, but she was never certain if he were the fisherman or the fishing line itself moving through space, landing gently on the water over and over, patiently waiting for a strike.

As quickly as Hugo had drifted, he returned as quickly with conviction.

"Alfred Kleinen's story is a story about who was responsible, *is* responsible." Hugo looked at Carmen with certainty and went on. "Look at it this way, whether a farmer's wife falls down a cliff or a Chinese kitchen boy tumbles off a pier—"

"Or a whale gets hit by a ship?"

"Exactly, or a whale gets hit by a ship," he smiled. "These events are never isolated. Something or someone sets them in motion; someone or something is responsible. Do you see?"

"I'm afraid I don't. Go on."

"Alfred was *supposed to* see the dead kitchen boy on his way home from the bar, just like the blue whale was *supposed to* make landfall exactly where she did."

Carmen was intrigued.

"I'm still in the dark here. Hugo, you're going to have to start at the beginning."

26

It was a rare Sunday when Sara would grace Otis Street. Her Sundays were reserved for Dunne family outings. That weekend, she had signed up the five of them for a salt marsh restoration project. When she fielded the call from the district attorney on her private line, Sara left her husband and two older kids at the Eco Center in Heron's Head Park for the shoreline cleanup along India Basin while she rushed to Otis Street with her youngest son George in tow.

The door to Otis Street opened to a man, huffing and puffing.

"Elevator out?" Sara asked indifferently.

"Cardio," he announced. "But I think they cut the air on weekends." Sara waited for Joseph Ryan, San Francisco's current district attorney, to catch his breath and guzzle a bottled water from her office fridge.

"What's 'cardio' mean?" George asked in his angelic voice, breaking away from looking at the news clippings tacked to the scrapbook on Hugo's office wall.

The little voice from Hugo's inner sanctum startled the DA. "Who is that? I thought we were alone."

"He's my son George; he's five." George had recently discovered the endless joy of questions. George quickly lost interest in the wall art and moved into the front office, testing the operative features of the office door along the way. He discovered that the ornate Victorian brass knob snapped back every time to his satisfaction.

"Did you know that a blue whale spends most of its day underwater?" asked George in all innocence.

DA Ryan, suited in jogging shorts and a Stanford jersey, made the mistake of replying in an impatient tone. "No, I didn't."

Dismissing George, the DA went on to explain to Sara how her boss was dangerously coloring outside the lines *again.* "In the first place, Inspector Sandoval has no authority in Mendocino County," Ryan said before rambling on about the intricacies of law enforcement protocols and inter-departmental cooperation. He ended the lecture by placing a sealed dark brown unmarked file folder on Sara's desk.

"Mom, how old do whales get?"

Before the DA left Otis Street, he delivered a warning. "Sara, this comes from the top. Sandoval is to stop making inquiries into the death of Jack Dillon. It's an order."

"Ordered by whom?"

"This is serious, Sara. This is all he gets. I shouldn't even be giving him this," Ryan pointed to the folder. "Just get the word to Hugo. Call off Harrison or someone is going to get hurt up there," warned Ryan, earbuds dangling from around his neck. The DA slammed the door behind him to underscore his point.

"Whatever you say, Joey." Sara opened the folder, barely comforted in the knowledge that the District Attorney was two steps behind. *One*, he could have easily messengered the file over but whoever got to him insisted he deliver it personally (probably the mayor, as she and Hugo were still in the honeymoon phase); *and two*, the DA had no idea that someone had already been hurt.

The contents of the folder were revealing. The chief and T. Ray were on to something. Three pages, and *two* reports of Jack Dillon's fatal accident the night he wrapped his 2005 Tundra truck around a lone cypress on Highway 1 at Ten Mile. One was from the Highway Patrol with the autopsy report attached and one from the Sheriff's office in Mendocino County. Both reports described the scene: tire tracks, direction, estimated speed at impact—and both confirmed that the alcohol found on the interior of the pickup truck and on Jack Dillon's body originated from the broken whiskey bottle in the truck cab. But that's where agreement between the reports ended.

Deputy Sheriff A. Ruiz was first on the scene and indicated the incident was an auto accident involving a drunk driver, while the Highway Patrol's report listed the incident as suspicious, deferring to the medical examiner's autopsy which clearly stated that no whiskey or alcohol of any kind was found in Jack Dillon's system.

"So, this is why you told me that you were never here, eh, Mr. Ryan?" Sara began to text her boss.

"What, Mom? Who's Mister Ryan?" George put his arm around her waist.

"No one to worry about, George. He won't be re-elected," she said, looking down at her baby. "We'll get going soon, okay?"

"Mom, is Dad going to take us out in the boat after we clean up the Bay?"

Ping.

Sara looked down at her text, "Yes, darling, but first I need to figure out who Gertrude is."

27

DAN MERTEN, THE SHERIFF OF MENDOCINO COUNTY, looked across his beaten-up, battle-scarred, institutional desk at the Fort Bragg Substation at T. Ray slumped in a worn club chair.

"Someone sank the *Tango II* in the harbor last night," the sheriff said in a business-like tone. "You wouldn't have any idea who could have possibly drilled a hole from under the bow, now would you, Ray?"

T. Ray knew Dan was a tough, no-nonsense sheriff, but sending a pair of deputies to fetch him from his home at dawn seemed a bit reckless, not to mention rude, under the circumstances. Without a warrant, it was a long shot that he would have gone with the detectives willingly, but the sheriff was betting on T. Ray's good-natured curiosity.

"Look, the last thing my head needs this morning are stupid questions, Dan. I might have been clocked hard yesterday, but when they peeled me off the deck of that fishing boat I'm guessing the Coast Guard would have noticed if she were on the bottom. Those Coasties down in Noyo are pretty sharp," he shot back.

"Why did you go down in the harbor?" One of Dan's deputies fetched a cup of coffee for the guest.

"I wanted some chowder but Sally's was closed."

"Why did you board the *Tango II*?"

"I know the captain. He wasn't there. I'm not saying he was with Sally, but you never know. Small town and all," said T. Ray. "Look, what am I doing here, Dan?"

"I had a tip you went *back* to the harbor last night."

"I was home, with my wife, until your boys showed up," said T. Ray, rubbing his sore head.

Shuffling through the incident report, the sheriff summarized for T. Ray "The Coast Guard report says that despite your injuries you refused medical attention at the scene. It also says here you could barely stand and that a friend of yours helped you into your truck and the two of you drove off."

"If they say so."

"Who drove you to the Lost Pub?

"No idea. I was pretty out of it."

"This your knife?"

"Yeah, I've been looking for that," he laughed.

"It was sitting on the seat of your truck. Looks like 'T II' is carved on the handle."

"Actually, I'm Thelonious the *Third* but I ran out of room on the knife."

"Who drove you in your truck to the pub last night, Ray?"

"I really don't know. What I do know is my wife drove me home and, somehow, she got me into bed before I passed out. Are we done here?" With some difficulty T. Ray gestured to the non-uniformed man lurking behind him. "Before I go, who the hell is this guy?"

"This *guy* is DEA," said the no-name Fed in a voice as gray as his suit. "Satellite picked up a grow in the forest on the Dillon Ranch, Mr. Harrison. Good size, too, maybe 2,000 plants."

"Got a name?"

"Weeks. Special Agent Weeks."

The sheriff decided to get between them. "Look, Ray, the raid is going down this morning, thanks to your chief tipping us off, and we're grateful. I don't have all the pieces yet so if you remember anything from last night, you call me."

"Good to know we're all caught up. But why haul me in? You know damn well I didn't sink that boat." T. Ray snapped, still a little hot.

"You're here primarily because I want you to keep your friends away from the ruckus today. That includes Sandoval, his daughter, the whole crew. Christ almighty, Ray, my boys tell me the cove is already a circus this morning. Just keep your people contained out there. But most importantly keep the Dillon family inside the house."

"The Dillons are just two people, Dan, and one of them is in her nineties. Hell, she can't weigh more than a hundred pounds, maybe hundred ten soaking wet."

"That may be. Don't underestimate her, Ray. She's a force of nature."

"So I've heard."

"Look, I'll deputize you if you like but I'm counting on you to keep her away from the raid. It's for her own good. I'll come by the farm when it's all over."

"Cate Dillon is important to a lot of important people on this coast. Don't you worry, we'll keep her safe," promised T. Ray. Sheriff Dan's concern for Cate Dillon's welfare was genuine enough but T. Ray also knew it was *not* for her own good. "Oh, and it's a hard pass on the badge. By the way, Dan, did you ever find Ruiz?" He dug at the sheriff with a crooked smile.

T. Ray's question ironed out any creases left in the sheriff's uniform. The sheriff spat out. "We found his patrol car stashed in a shed on the ranch. He's up in the forest tending to his crop, I suspect."

The DEA agent added, "Harrison, you might think you're a tough guy right about now, but you got lucky yesterday. It's a good thing those guys who jumped you on the boat were scared off; could have been fatal. We haven't caught them yet but when we do, I suspect we'll find out they work for the cartel."

"Cartel, hell. It's just local boys trying to make a living," said T. Ray. He could see the sheriff was on the fence about it.

"Don't be too sure about that. Someone is behind Ruiz, someone or something big," warned the agent. "Cartels are like rattlesnakes; they hide in the shadows. That is, until they are forced to strike," he added, before pulling the sheriff into a side conference.

T. Ray had found the agent's folksy analogy both unexpected and overly dramatic. In response, he placed the ice pack back where it belonged, on his ribs. Somehow Daisy had slipped it to him between shouting at the deputies who claimed they were only helping her husband into the back seat of their patrol car. Sinking down in the sheriff's office chair, T. Ray closed what his wife called his *baby blues* and let the ice pack do its thing.

It surprised him what came to mind while he drifted—the peeling 1880s farmhouse with a widow's walk on the roof above the Queen Anne turret. That's when he imagined—or remembered—how the reflection of an old woman in the curved glass was framed in lace curtains on the top floor.

So this is why Sandoval does this. He sees visions!

"I'll be damned," he said out loud. He might as well have shouted, "Eureka!" or had a lightbulb go on over his head.

"What is it, Harrison?" asked the DEA agent.

"Can I go now?" T. Ray pointed to his throbbing head. He needed to get to Hugo before all hell broke loose.

"Unless you have something more you want to tell us," said Sheriff Dan.

"Dan, I'm not going to corral the Dillon family for you."

"Thought I'd give it a shot," the sheriff confessed.

"Harrison, if I find you're withholding evidence or any information about the raid which might assist my team, you'll be right back in here," bullied Weeks, suspicious.

Looking at the federal agent sideways, the sheriff concluded. "Thanks for comin' in, Ray. I'll have a deputy take you home."

Daisy, who had skirted past more than one deputy, burst into the sheriff's office unannounced. "That won't be necessary, Dan. I've got this."

28

THE BLUE WAS ALMOST UNRECOGNIZABLE, her remains wedged in the tidepools bordered on the surreal. The defleshing phase—the cutting away the blubber and flesh—was a turbulent scene in dramatic contrast to the pastoral marine life clinging to the walls around what was left of the rotting whale.

At first light, dozens of volunteers and marine scientists had gathered on the cliffs overlooking Chicken Cove for the ceremony, and more were arriving each hour. While the necropsy phase had ended with the whale's precious organs shipped to research facilities around the globe, the work of deconstructing the blue whale was far from over. To save the skeleton for the town, Ava and her team would need luck.

Five days before the return of the high tides. Just five days to remove tons of the mother whale's flesh from her bones and lifted off the sands, hoisted up the cliff to waiting trucks. In that narrow window, every inch of the ninety-foot blue whale would need to be cleaned and labeled before the skeleton could be salvaged. The plan was to truck the bones to a secret gravesite in the Mendocino forest, where the final decomposition would take place over years, but the destination of the blubber had not yet been resolved. The only processors that could manage it would face stiff fines for commercializing a federally protected species.

Hugo sat cross-legged well back from the edge of the cliff comfortably at his side on one of the short lawn chairs Ava had set out for VIPs.

"You could have given me more of a warning, Hugo. I must look a fright. I barely had time to brush my teeth."

"I knew you wouldn't want to miss this," Hugo said as the Yurok elder started singing the blessing from the beach below. "Besides," he said, looking up at her. "You look lovely."Carmen smiled gratefully back at Hugo. The night before, they found that the twenty feet of hallway separating their rooms at the Lost Inn held fast, but she wondered for how long? Carmen knew very well why she had left her husband sixteen months before, it was jealousy— and not of another woman, but of his City.

Hugo watched Carmen close her eyes to add her own private blessing to the Yuroks' chanting below.

When she opened them, she whispered to the man under the Borsalino, "You know who did this, don't you?" Carmen said.

"Sure. It was an accident, a ship strike," he replied without editorial, and flipped his brim back.

"You know that's not what I'm talking about. You've figured out who set this in motion—the cannabis, the red tag on the cottage. I can read you, Hugo, always could. You know, don't you?"

He looked at her, then away. "Yes."

"Oh, dear, why do I fear this is going to be a heartbreaker?" She hoped Nate wasn't involved.

The Airstream's shiny silver door swung open. Lobo was the first to thunder out, followed by Nate, then Ava, who called her dog back inside with a whistle.

"Good morning, sleepy heads, you're missing this," whispered Carmen, for Ava's benefit.

"Give me a break, Mom. I've been up for hours. I had to take a shower, I was covered in whale," Ava ran her fingers through still-damp hair.

"Nate," Hugo called him over quietly. "I want you to check in on your gran right away. Stay with her at the house until I can get there. And don't take the tunnel; cut over the highway." Nate gave Ava a quick kiss and without delay, jogged across the land toward the highway and farmhouse beyond.

Ava, happy as a child, squeezed in between her parents near the cliff as if they were on a family adventure, watching the ceremony below.

Just then T. Ray and Daisy drove in and parked, followed by an armada of law enforcement vehicles. Bringing up the rear, The Joe's mobile coffee truck Joe on the Go.

Favoring his bruised ribs, T. Ray eased down next to Hugo while Daisy sat with Carmen and Ava.

"You're never going to believe this," Daisy started in. "The sheriff got an anonymous tip that T. Ray sank a fishing boat in the harbor last night. Dan sent two of his deputies to the house to drag my sweet man to the station. It was still dark, for god sakes!" Daisy said loudly, hoping Sheriff Dan would hear.

Hugo remarked, "Only two?" Carmen and Ava laughed.

"Hey, Ava, we passed Nate crossing the road; he was practically running. Where is he off to?" T. Ray said to Ava. "And did anyone call Eli?" he asked the lineup, wanting to close the loops.

Ping.

Hugo glanced at his phone before turning to Carmen, "I'll be right back," and headed to the coffee truck where the sheriff was waiting for his order.

"Bring me a latte, would you, darling?" Carmen called after him. Ava smiled at her mother, wondering if the *darling* was casual or intentional.

At Joe on the Go, Hugo ordered a Cubano and a latte before

showing his phone with the latest text from Otis Street to the sheriff.

6:45 a / Coast Guard chased down a small fishing boat off Mendocino coast with your Capt. Henshaw on board —SD

The sheriff nodded. "Thought Skip might run. It's old-school using boats to move product, but I can see why they would try it. The cove is perfect. It would have worked, too, had that whale not parked it. Chief, a few minutes ago DEA picked up Skip's son Moses at his grandmother's trailer over in Willits. The kid confessed everything, including the name of the supply ship that would take the crop from the *Tango II* to market. As we speak, the Coast Guard is in a hot chase to intercept the ship before it leaves U.S. territorial waters."

"Nice," Hugo said, satisfied. "But who told Moses the name of the ship? Who hired them?"

Sheriff Merten shook off the answer and backed away from the coffee truck, inviting Hugo to follow. "Everybody wants into the game. Cannabis might be the only crop that saves this county, but why the Dillons?" he whispered, genuinely distraught.

Hugo admired Mendocino's long, unruly coastline and impenetrable forests, where the sheriff often had to balance conflicting county and federal laws. Eli had told Hugo that the sheriff had introduced an innovative program to license medical marijuana grows in the county, a program designed to ensure the safety of all citizens in his county, but it angered the Feds.

"The DEA is assigned to look for large commercial grows on National Forest land, but these small farms are fair game—that is if the DEA can find them," said the sheriff.

Hugo was sympathetic. "For the grower, it would be a good bet that the small grow on the Dillon Ranch would slip through their net. They just couldn't have figured on a blue whale getting in the way."

"Unfortunately, we're under attack by drug traffickers up here. We have thousands of illegal grows in my county but this one you brought to us is unique in its conspiracy—the intent to sell, multiple counts of fraud, intimidation, and I suspect even murder. To top it off, this is personal; it involves one of my own." Sheriff Dan shook his head. Anyone could see the man was tired.

"Home-grown, 100 percent local—at least that's what the billboard up the road says," Hugo mused.

The sheriff chuckled. "Agent Weeks is going to be severely disappointed when this raid doesn't lead him to a cartel. You should have heard Ray set him straight this morning."

Hugo smiled but, like the sheriff's laughter, it was lukewarm.

* * *

With their paddles up and the faithful lining the Cove, the Yurok blessing floated up on the thermals and soared with a squadron of pelicans. Latte in hand, Carmen turned her back on the ceremony to watch her ex-husband strike out on a mission, Borsalino squared. From the cliff, she couldn't possibly see the widow's walk of the Dillon farmhouse peeking through the Cypress grove, much less the shadows that clouded Hugo's face as he crossed the coast road. She took no pleasure in knowing she had guessed it.

It was going to be a heartbreaker.

29

SINCE HIS FIRST VIEW OF THE FARMHOUSE, Hugo had been struck by the less than elegant front entry. Compared to classic Victorians in the City, this one appeared to be a hybrid. He guessed its presentation was due to the altered years after the house was built in the 1880s. The building inspector went on to suspect the original veranda had once been more expansive. Likely replaced in the 1920s or even later, the veranda was shortened to accommodate the large, rounded turret which had been added to the southwest corner in the elaborate Queen Anne-style. Hugo speculated the original owner, Nate's notorious lumber baron, might have added the formal feature to his front parlor to satisfy a fancy new wife, or added it later to show off his wealth to passersby on the then-new coast road.

From the parlor, the dowager listened as Nate spoke with someone on the short porch. Peering through lace curtains, she could trace Hugo's solemn form as he approached her door.

"Come in, come in, Inspector," she prompted. "Please come in and sit with me," she added in a strong but gracious voice. Nate left Hugo with Cate and headed back across the road.

Cate was a living flashback to another century, perfectly framed in the parlor's light blue cornflower wallpaper. It appeared to Hugo that the room's delicate chandeliers and ornate rugs suspended time beneath the parlor's robin's-egg-blue ceiling that watched over her.

"I've been wondering, Mrs. Dillon, when was the turret added? It's magnificent, but that style came along much later than this Victorian," Hugo opened.

"You have a fine eye, Inspector," she said, looking over his shoulder to the obstructed view beyond the curved glass. "It was a gift from Big JD to his new bride. We were married in 1945. My husband had already begun the work on the turret long before they raised the roadbed." Then she adding with cynicism, "The *Great Highway* Project."

"But that was in 1939," Hugo guessed.

"Well, yes. It was 1939 in Southern California but here in the north, the project came much later. Before the highway was straightened and raised, the coast road wandered in and around our creeks. We had an unobstructed view of the ocean from where we are sitting right now. I can still see the blue from the top floor, but I don't climb the stairs any longer." She went on, her sadness mixed with bitterness, "When 'progress' arrived, it was without so much as a knock at the door. Today, our view is reserved for strangers passing through."

With the small talk out of the way, the matriarch proceeded with the business at hand.

"*He* was unexpected as well, Inspector," she said, nodding in the direction of the cove where Nate had disappeared beyond the roadbed. Suddenly overwhelmed, the weary farmer's wife sank into the flowery, overstuffed chair. Hugo thought the chair would devour her, but the old woman remained resolute, her back straight.

"I love him, but he's not mine," she confessed. Her bright eyes turned a gray like the sleet that covers the road ahead. Seeing through it, she went on. "His mum, Grace, was like a daughter to me. When Nate was born, he was most decidedly born a Dillon. It's just that he's not my son's boy. Understand what I am telling you, Inspector. The ranch is his, all of it. I made certain after Big J.D. passed that Nathanial inherits everything when I die, despite any questions which might arise over his birthright."

Hugo remained respectfully silent.

"I want you to know the boy knew nothing about the crop my son was planting," she insisted.

"Mrs. Dillon, how did you get involved in this?" Hugo asked gently.

"Jack never wanted this for his son, you know."

"Take me to the beginning, Mrs. Dillon. I know you didn't start this."

"My, my, Inspector, you *are* direct. I can see how you hunger to inspect every inch of this Victorian, and now me in it." Cate rose from her chair to pour tea. "I think you are a rare combination, a modern man with the *patience* for an old woman."

Tea served, she sat again, ready to unburden her story at last. "One day, about this time last year, my old foreman came up to the house. He knew the ranch was in trouble and he told me he had found a way out."

"Andy Ruiz. That's right, he was your ranch foreman until he became a deputy sheriff."

Cate nodded. "Andy was with us for twenty years. My son Jack was never a rancher. Jack's father could do it all before the stroke. Honestly, I don't know how we would have survived without Andy after Big JD fell ill. Jack had gone to war, you see, but when my son returned, the farm was in trouble. Jack blamed Andy and left him no choice but to leave the ranch."

"Go on."

"Last winter when Andy stood where you are sitting now and handed me a cashier's check for $50,000. He promised to bring more to pay off the loans and free the ranch of all debt. I was shocked. I asked him where he got that kind of money, and he told me that he had friends who wanted to farm the land up the hill between the two creeks. When I questioned who his friends were and what they wanted to farm, he told me to speak to Jack."

"So Jack knew of the plan to grow cannabis."

Cate almost laughed. "Jack was in the parlor the entire time. He was sitting by the fireplace, just there. He kept his back to me when Andy handed me the check. After Andy left, Jack said the deal had been made and there was no going back. I pleaded with him, but he was as stubborn as his old man and would not reconsider."

Hugo saw that the story was taking its toll on the old woman. But like waves crashing, there was a force behind her.

"As I say, I was shocked. For months Jack had supported my decision to bring in the Land Trust to take over so we could live out our lives on the ranch in peace. Then out of the blue, he makes a deal with the devil. Jack insisted we didn't need the Land Trust, that he wanted to keep the ranch in the family for his son."

It was impossible for Hugo not to notice. It wasn't age or heartache, something else was weighing on Cate Dillon.

"Time went by, then suddenly Jack had this crazy idea to grow hops instead of cannabis." Her voice dropped to a whisper. "We had already taken so much money and it was time to plant."

"You said Jack was a terrible farmer," Hugo prompted.

"I warned him hops would never take hold, but he kept insisting he could turn the dairy barn into a brewery. It was the way out, he said. It was all Jack talked about. He even started to convert the barn." Cate took a break from her story to take her tea. One of Hugo's gifts was patience, but he was starting to get edgy; the clock was ticking.

"Jack was going to plant hops and nothing else. The dairy barn was full of thousands of cannabis seedlings; I begged him to plant them. *It was what we were paid to do*, I told him, but my son wouldn't listen. When the investor found out he was furious. Jack had already driven the plants out to his beach cottage—he called them his 'hostages'—and threatened to burn the cottage to the ground and the seedlings with it if this guy didn't back off."

It made a twisted sense to Hugo. Why hadn't he seen it sooner?

Only a skilled carpenter could have removed the floorboards and thresholds in the beach cottage with such precision. Hugo was chilled to think of Jack staging his own beloved cottage to burn.

"The investor came up to the house and demanded I talk sense into my son. I tried to convince him that Jack was bluffing. I told him my son would never burn down the cottage he had built for *her*." Cate stopped to catch her breath and go on. "It was the following night Jack's truck hit the tree up at Ten Mile. And then he was gone."

Cate sat silently, holding her hand to her breast; the ticking of a clock filled the room while distant waves caressed the shore.

"A tragic loss; I am truly sorry," Hugo expressed his condolences. He could see that Cate had started to drift, but he needed more from her.

"Who is Jack's investor?"

"Truth was my son didn't die up at Ten Mile. Jack had been dead for years. He died the day Grace went over the cliff."

"I need to ask, Mrs. Dillon—where did the money come from?" Hugo pressed gently.

"The money," the old woman almost smiled. "The money kept coming in like clockwork after Jack died and I did nothing to stop it, did I? My only worry was if Nathaniel found out he might go away for good. It was all cash, Inspector. I took it to keep the ranch for Nate. The boy has lost so much."

"Cate! The name." Hugo took her hand.

"Fitzpatrick," she said, without further hesitation. "Dustin Connor Fitzpatrick."

Hugo was stunned. The chill returned.

"Now my boy is buried next to his pa up on the hill, right below where that jackal Fitz is farming his weed for money."

"*He be waitin for the floores I be bringin from the gairden,*" Cate said to herself, envisioning the stones lined up inside the iron surround behind the farmhouse—her husband, her daughter-in-law, her son, with room for her.

The Scottish lass pulled her hand away. "What a waste, all those years, all that sweat—and now to end so badly. The ranch fed half the Coast through the Depression and the tough years that followed. So many of the families have left the Coast. Ah, who even remembers?"

Hugo felt like a priest taking a confession. "What went wrong?"

"Besides your daughter's whale beaching in the Cove?" This time, Cate did laugh. "Tell me, Inspector, how did you know I was involved?"

"I listened. Every time your name came up, I was told how you know everything that moves on this coast. Believe me, Mrs. Dillon, I have no idea how deep you're in this and, if I were being honest, I don't want to know. But you told Ruiz to post the red tag on the beach cottage. You must have thought that would keep Nate away from the cove when they moved the cannabis to the boat. Am I close?"

She nodded. "You pieced this all together from the red tag? I am impressed, Inspector. You are a dark horse, lad." Cate sat as straight in her chair as ever, but she seemed lighter with the burden shifted off her weary shoulders.

As Hugo stood to leave, Cate caught his hand. "Don't make this your last visit, Hugo." she said with difficulty.

While the old woman's blue eyes danced for him one more time, Hugo saw how her wrinkled hand gripped the door frame for strength.

30

T. Ray had caught up to Hugo outside the farmhouse after dodging a line of cars and pickup trucks slowing on the highway to turn not into the headlands but down to the Dillon homestead where they parked one by one under the cypress trees.

T. Ray could see Hugo was puzzled.

"I spoke to the gal with the two little girls over there. Every year, they come to sit with your Cate on the anniversary of her husband's death; something about repaying an old debt."

They stood back as the vehicles released a flood of women and children, carrying baskets filled with food and flowers bound for the farmhouse.

Hugo imagined that these were the very neighbors Cate thought had forgotten her and wondered how many of them shared tattoos with her and the waitress at the Blue Crab. If Sara's information was correct, it was not long after Nate's mother Grace fell down the cliff that a local fishing boat sank off Chicken Point taking its crew with her. The boat's name was the *Gertrude*, a great loss to the community Hugo had come to respect.

"Sandoval, the guy watching the Lost Pub wasn't there about the ADA access. Fitz was fooled; the dude was with the DEA,"

T. Ray announced.

"And what does that tell you, Harrison?"

"It tells me Fitz is in the business of selling more than beer." It gnawed on T. Ray that Hugo was always more than a few steps ahead of him and especially that morning with his head splitting.

Hugo looked over to his bruised partner, then beckoned him to the backside of the farmhouse. Hanging from the second-floor balcony railing was a dripping wetsuit.

"I'm guessing that's the balcony off Nate's room," Hugo said.

"The balls on that kid, Sandoval. How do you think Nate made the connection to the *Tango II*?"

"Nate did say he was down on the beach Thursday morning like every morning. He didn't want to tell us, but he must have seen Moses return for his ropes."

"But is that enough reason to sink her? Like the man said, your future son-in-law might have just poked a rattlesnake."

"God, I hope not."

"Hey. Sandoval, you, okay?"

They were halfway to the tunnel before Hugo could tell him. "It was Jack who set this all up. Ruiz definitely had his hand in it, but it was Jack who made the deal."

Despite the Sheriff's warning, they took the shortcut. Still in the light, T. Ray asked, "She a part of this?" jerking his head at the farmhouse.

Hugo nodded. Eighty feet of silence followed. When the light hit them again, the roar of the sea muffled in the tunnel was released. It took Hugo only a few strides in the open to bring T. Ray up to speed on the story Cate had just told him.

"Jack and Fitz were partners. When Jack got cold feet about the cannabis and tried to switch to hops, Fitz wouldn't go along. That's when Jack took the plants hostage," Hugo told his partner.

"So it was Jack who was getting the beach cottage ready to burn. If he was afraid of Fitz, that explains the guns, I guess."

"I think Jack was honestly trying to save his ranch, and things got out of hand." Hugo held his Borsalino to his head as the wind kicked up.

"Does Cate think Fitz has anything to do with her son's so-called accident?"

"I didn't have the heart to go there. I even wanted her to stop talking but she kept going. She said she knew who I was and what I had to do, but the trouble is, Harrison, *I* don't know what I have to do."

T. Ray could no longer hear his friend as a trio of black helicopters broke through the sky over the headlands.

"Showtime," T. Ray shouted, "Let's go!"

The men ran across the open grassland towards the Airstream and the Cove. The circus the Sheriff had predicted was well underway. Hugo wondered how Sunday could have taken such a hard turn.

It had begun peacefully enough with his daughter's hand in his as they watched the Yurok ceremony from the cliff at dawn. Their hearts kept time with the drum of the elders who sang to the spirit of the whale. When the morning light had filled the cove, they watched as nearly twenty kayaks floated between the breakers and the beach, paddles raised.

The peace at sunrise had turned to an intense, orchestrated production in the Cove. The first act, the deconstruction of the whale, in its third day. The Yurok's experience and tools had proved invaluable to all the volunteers, while the elders took advantage of the event to train their youth in tribal traditions. Although the Yurok prize whales for food, the tribe does not hunt them, but only harvest "drift whales," the ones that wash up on the shore. The blue in Chicken Cove was such a whale.

The second act of the morning in Chicken Cove was the hoisting of the blubber, bucket by bucket, followed by the third act of transport. Lucky for all, a crane company showed up that morning, completely out of the blue. Its owner had heard on the radio about how the hoists by hand up the cliff were proving too slow and dangerous. After trial and error with a boom truck, the crane operator set up a double-bucket system custom-engineered to fly the rotting flesh into waiting trucks.

The pressure was on. Ava's team would have to complete the removal and tag the skeleton by the return of high tides in just six days. To add to the stress there was an early storm building over the Pacific which could make landfall even sooner. While Ava directed the activity in the Cove, Nate monitored from the cliffs with clipboard and walkie-talkie. It was the young Dillon's job to keep a record of the blubber piling up on the trailers. Carmen spoke to the media for Ava. Meanwhile, the volunteers funneled in via Daisy and, though it wasn't the entire town as she'd proclaimed in the pub, the turnout was impressive.

T. Ray and Hugo arrived huffing from their jog to find Nate and Eli standing awkwardly next to each other near the trailers. Side by side, any stranger could see the resemblance between them.

"It was Nate here who came up with this hoist and bucket system," Hugo bragged to Eli. "*Brilliant*, as Carmen would say."

"Eli, you ought to ask Nate about the old doghole ports," T. Ray chimed in. "In fact, it was Nate who called in the historian from the State Parks to help with some old photographs of the port back in the day. I honestly couldn't picture how it was going to work; even the crane owner said he could never have figured it out without the photographs."

T. Ray gave the embarrassed Nate an encouraging slap on his shoulder. "Why don't you walk the mayor out to the beach cottage and show him some of your art while he's here? I'll take over for you."

"And while you're out there, you might want to tell Mayor Callaghan about last night," suggested Hugo, looking to Nate with confidence.

Eli nodded. "Sounds great. Would you grab us a couple coffees, Nate? I'll just be a minute here with the chief. Tell Bella to put it all on my tab."

The mayor took Hugo aside. "You staying over, Chief? I hear you can't go back to your room at the Inn. I want you to know you're always welcome to stay with us if the Harrisons are booked up."

"No. I'm afraid I need to get back to the City, but I might take you up on that sometime, Eli. I do appreciate it. And for god sakes, call me Hugo."

"Next time then, Hugo," he paused, overwhelmed. "Anytime. And I'll keep an eye on Cate for you; I'll do my best to keep her out of the deep end of this if I can. As for my son—," and with that Eli's eyes clouded; he was truly out of words. Suddenly Hugo did a rare thing, he allowed Eli to hug him.

Nate came back with two coffees; father and son turned and walked together toward the Point. When the pair were well out of earshot, T. Ray asked, "Sandoval, why didn't you tell me about Fitz earlier?"

"I had no idea it was Fitz until this morning," Hugo confessed.

"Damn. It was Fitz all along. He paid off the liens on the ranch and funneled the hush money to Cate, and it was Fitz who hired the *Tango II* to pick up the crop in Chicken Cove and deliver it to the supply ship offshore."

"He hatched quite a plan," Hugo agreed, "but it wasn't Fitz who told Ruiz to post the red tag; that was Cate trying to protect her grandson. And it wasn't Fitz who told Skip to get rid of the whale; that had to be Ruiz. No, this Fitz character is too smart to panic. When the whale got in the way and Ruiz bungled it, he just shifted to his Plan B."

T. Ray tried to stretch out his injured shoulder while they watched the black helicopters circle the ranch, hovering in formation over the forest. "What *is* his Plan B, Chief?"

"Wait for it," smiled Hugo as he studied the cuts and bruises on T. Ray's face. The new marks pushed aside scars from previous encounters and once healed, would hardly be noticed.

Hugo pointed to the forested hills above the farmhouse where the family plot rested below the field of cannabis concealed in the trees. From the Airstream, he and T. Ray watched the DEA raid unfold from a comfortable distance. It was intimidating. The black helicopters worked the raid as if herding the fleet below out of the woods—armed black SUVs on all sides of a large panel truck followed by several men on foot zip-tied to each other.

"Plan B was to transport the crop in that refrigerated seafood truck so no one would think twice when it pulled into the harbor near the *Tango II*. That's why you got clunked, Harrison."

"I'll be damned."

31

WITH FITZ'S DOGS AT HIS HEELS, Hugo wandered the streets of the old company town searching for cell phone reception. Traversing the crooked alleyways, he tempted the Fates who lingered after their ride on the economic slide that had nearly buried the coastal town two years before. In the long shadows of the afternoon, strange voices and darting figures spun out of gamey wood-clad buildings long abandoned, but Hugo wasn't thrown. Instead, he had come to see Fort Bragg as a true frontier town, a bit ragged around the edges but strong in its core and scored with a defiant sense of adventure and promise. It reminded him of parts of the Southern Waterfront in San Francisco, where a bit of wildness still survived along the Bay.

In front of the free-standing garage with *NO BARKING* scrawled in blue paint on its door, Hugo made the phone connection with Otis Street. Not comfortable with the Bluetooth, he kept the cell phone to his ear and planted his feet.

Sara was excited. "Chief, not only has the discovery of the little blue bottle stopped the eviction of the Two Bits Bar + Grill but the mayor was so impressed with our report that she called for an emergency Board of Supes meeting to review the condition of the seawall."

Part of Hugo's survival at the department was his skepticism. "Why this overwhelming response?"

"Apparently, it's not the history of the bottle itself, but where you found on the surface of the seawall where an artifact of this age shouldn't be. At your suggestion, I asked for comments from all in the boat to include in the report. Turns out it was the civil engineer from the Port who nailed it, and I quote, "*The discovery of this bottle is evidence that the seawall is far more fragile than realized.*"

"Mike Shreck. I should have guessed," Now Hugo was smiling. "Great work, No. 1. I'll be back in action tomorrow. Anything else for me?"

"The Estuary Report we've been waiting for came out Friday. I had them send over a hard copy; it's on your desk." Sara's voice came in clear until he started to walk. "You still there, Chief? One more thing. David Marino at the Port called; he wants you to investigate tenant complaints on Pier 45. Should we bring in Mr. Harrison?"

"No, not just yet. Harrison has an assignment up here while he's recovering. And Sara, I may not be in the office for a few days."

"Right Chief. I'll set the meeting for later in the week. I should mention that Rocco—"

"Let me guess, Rocco wants to come along."

Sara's laughter was drowned out by a seagull calling from the rooftop. When the dogs started barking, Hugo had to hang up. *I guess dogs can't read*, he thought.

Out front of the Lost Inn and Pub, Hugo found T. Ray, Daisy and Carmen taking turns leaning on patrol cars and lampposts while they waited for the all-clear.

"They're still in there," Daisy informed Hugo upon his return.

The *they* Daisy referred to was a small army of DEA agents along with the sheriff's team combing the premises for evidence of drug trafficking. Even the state's Alcoholic Beverage Control wanted in on the game.

"Perhaps the agents will do your laundry while they're at it,"

Carmen took a shot as she eyed Hugo in a rare, crumpled shirt.

"Good call. I could use a change before we head home. If I'm not mistaken, I believe Sara packed extras."

"Of course, she did," quipped Carmen, raising her eyebrows. It would be weeks before Hugo would learn that it was Carmen who was the one who had told Sara to prepare the go bag.

"This is silly. Just because your rooms are locked off, it doesn't mean you have to leave," pleaded Daisy. "Stay a few days with us; it's been too long. It will be fun and there's plenty of room."

"You know I'd love to darling, but Hugo's my ride. Aren't you, Hugo?" Carmen looked hopefully at her ex. It was a good excuse to get out of blubber duty.

"You want a ride? What happened to your helicopter?" Hugo teased. "Daisy, I really do need to get back. I just spoke with Sara, and she told me Rocco is up in arms over a complaint on Pier 45—that's where the herring boats bring in their catch. And there's a public meeting for herring permits this week. I want to look in on him before it all hits."

"That hearing isn't scheduled for another *two* weeks," corrected Carmen.

"How in the world do you know that?" Hugo said taking a step back.

"I spoke to Rocco yesterday. He talked me into representing the herring fishery in the Gashouse Cove lawsuit and the permits came up."

Hugo raised his eyebrows under the Borsalino. "You're representing the fishery? Really?" Hugo had to smile when he imagined the number of phone calls Carmen was in for.

"We will be back soon, I promise, Daisy. Keep an eye on Ava for us?" Carmen asked. Daisy put a reassuring arm around her best friend.

We, us? Daisy shot a look at her husband, who hadn't missed the use of the pronouns.

It was a good time for Hugo to change the subject. "I can't help but admire those doors." The inspector walked over to the pub's entrance to inspect the visible workings of the turnstile.

"Good eye, Sandoval, they sure would look swell down at Otis Street," T. Ray, egged him on.

"Don't indulge him," warned Carmen. "He already has the mayor sending him a chair."

Hugo looked to his ex-wife for a legal ruling. "With the liquor license in the wind, back taxes, fines, prison—I wonder what happens to these doors. I mean, do they become property of the state, or what?" Carmen let it slide.

"You might be able to pick them up at auction," goosed T. Ray, with a wink to Carmen.

Despite a minor hiccup when his sidearm got caught in the turn, Sheriff Dan emerged triumphantly through the coveted revolving doors.

"You can go up to your rooms now and gather your things. My office will be taking care of the bill," he announced.

"Dan, that's not necessary."

"It's the least I can do and, Chief, you know you're welcome in my county anytime. Oh, by the way, I called that idiot of a DA you have down there. He's all hung up about you roaming outside your jurisdiction. I told him you and Ray here have been acting as sworn deputies of the Mendocino County Sheriff's office and for him to back off."

"That works for us." Hugo reached for the sheriff's hand.

Carmen was not the only one surprised by Hugo's gesture. T. Ray rocked between astonishment and amusement; he could count the times Hugo had offered his hand.

"Maybe it's me, but there's something different about him," Daisy whispered to Carmen. "I can't put my finger on it, but I feel as if I am looking at a new, improved Hugo. What exactly happened last night?" Looking eagerly to her friend for the scoop, Daisy instead saw a wistfulness in Carmen's eyes as she watched her ex chat with the officers outside the doors in question.

* * *

The sea had started to kick up its skirt but the processing work in Chicken Cove continued unabated with the carcass well secured. On the open areas of the beach covered by tablecloths donated by a local restaurant, Ava's team sorted, wrapped, and coded each section of the skeleton. Three hundred and fifty-six bones, less the flippers. There was no need to label them, as, once scraped clean, the bones mirrored the human hand, all but the thumb.

At the Airstream Carmen and Hugo waited for their daughter who was busy on the beach directing the transfer of the calf's remains into the harness. All eyes focused on the clever Hawk Crane Company's boom as it gently hoisted the cradled specimen to the waiting flatbed for transport to the marine lab for a full necropsy. While the infant whale landed safely on the truck, Daisy dragged Carmen to the press tent for a quick interview. As the baby blue was being secured, Ava climbed the cliff and rushed to her father.

As she approached, Hugo saw a reflection of his own mother in Ava that he had never seen before. His heart stopped for a moment to make sense of it—more than her blue eyes, it was the strength he saw in them that was the connection. Named for Hugo's mother, a defiant Basque exile from the Spanish Pyrenees, Ava Rose was a beautiful name, they agreed, far prettier than the names Carmen could offer from her own grandmothers, Agnes and Harriet, Brits to the core.

Ava removed her rubberized gear splattered with whale before hugging her father. He was grateful for the consideration but was confused when she suddenly pulled away. "Dad, I know you've had your suspicions about Nate since you got here and, after last night's escapade, I don't blame you. Nate told me everything," Ava blurted.

"*Everything*?" Hugo thought. He knew Nate had more to tell his girlfriend than confessing to sinking a fishing boat.

Ava let loose. "He's not you, okay? He doesn't have it all figured out." She wiped a tear. "I don't either." Then she launched into a confession, "I have never, ever dismantled a blue whale. I don't even know if I can—."

He stopped her. "Pup, haven't you been telling me it's just like dissecting a big fish?"

Ava had to laugh at her father's stupid comment. When he joined in, she realized it had been a long time since her father called her by that nickname. She had been missing him.

"What's so funny, you two?" Carmen walked up.

"Nate told me that he sank the boat in the harbor last night and he's going to turn himself in," Ava announced after a big breath.

"Say again." Carmen looked over at Hugo who, to her surprise, did not appear to be concerned.

"Is Eli going with him?" Hugo asked Ava.

"Yes, thank god, the mayor has been very cool, very supportive," said Ava with some relief. "Also, I want you both to know Nate and I are very fond of each other; however, we have decided to take a break until we get our lives under control. No commitments just yet."

Carmen hugged her daughter. "I'm sorry it's not easy, darling. I wish we didn't have to leave, but your father has pressing business at Otis Street. We'll see you in the City in a couple of weeks, all right?"

"We?"

Carmen hugged her daughter again. "Shhh."

"Stop worrying, Mom. I don't think Uncle T is going to let me out of his sight until I'm back at the institute," Ava chuckled.

Ava held the door to the car for her father. As she planted a final kiss on his cheek, she whispered in his ear. "Remember, Dad, you promised."

32

THE BMW CONQUERED THE HEADLANDS one last time, skirting the fleet of cars while dodging the eager press and gently scattering spectators. Sporting his last clean white shirt, Hugo honked farewell at Ava and the barking Lobo tied up at the Airstream while Carmen waved from the passenger window.

Perhaps it was the mix of sea air combined with Carmen's bath soap that quieted their ride for the first ten miles.

"Hugo, do you think they'll look into Jack's accident?" She broke the ice.

"I think the mayor will insist, if only for his own peace of mind, not to mention his son's."

Hugo checked the rear view as bits of ranch mud continued to fly from the undercarriage of the once pristine sports car, splattering across the roadbed of Highway 1 South like a hailstorm. Pacing them, a formation of brown pelicans effortlessly dipped in and out of the coastline.

"How in the world did you figure Nate to be Eli's son?"

"It goes back to when I first saw the beach cottage. I could see the care and craftsmanship Jack put into the building. But for a happy family man, the location was too vulnerable, too remote. He could have put the cottage anywhere on the ranch, but he chose the cliffs. It was all wrong. I started to suspect Jack was hiding something."

"Nate would only have been a baby at the time. Maybe Jack thought he was losing her to Eli," Carmen said sadly. "Or had already lost her."

"Carmen, if you had been in the room when Eli was telling us the story of Grace falling to her death, you would have known right away. Eli's still in love with her, but I wasn't certain he had fathered Nate until last night in the pub."

"The hands?"

"Yep."

"I wonder if the boy knew before today?"

"I'm sure he suspected; he's a smart kid. Jack knew but the sad twist is Jack told his mother he was building the brewery for Nate; he loved him. When I looked in at the old creamery, I could see it was true. Jack had plans laid on his workbench and had already started to frame the decks to support the tanks."

Just then Carmen's cell phone rang. She turned it off with a dramatic flourish for Hugo's benefit. "It's that easy, darling. Pull over, I'm driving. You know I'm better behind the wheel."

As they neared the turn off to the freeway, Hugo did pull over, but only to give her the floor. "All right. Let's have it."

"Fine. All your stories last night about who is responsible, and today you're rushing back into her arms. Don't you see how far you've come? Hugo, look at what you can put in motion when you're free of the City. I don't understand you. How can you leave the Coast right now?"

"Carmen. There's nothing else for me to do here."

"What—this is about tying up loose ends, solving a puzzle? Hugo, this was never about the whale or even sorting out what happened on the ranch. Coming up here has always been about your daughter. This is her big moment; can't you see that?"

After a long wait for a response, she tacked on, "Lovely. And where does that leave us?"

Hugo looked at the dashboard, wondering if it was leather or not, before asking his passenger, "Carmen, you in a hurry to getback?"

"Not really," she said, without hesitation.

"Good," he said, turning the car around and driving north, *away* from his City.

"Now hold on, Hugo. Aside from Rocco, I know your waterfront is calling."

"The seawall report landed on the mayor's desk yesterday. She wants the Board of Supes to take a good look at it and that will take a few days to schedule. Meanwhile, Otis Street is filing a formal request with the Historic Preservation Commission to demand an investigation of the archeological artifacts buried in Sea Wall Lot 341. Sara's on top of it, Carmen. Not an hour ago, she told me that both the old and new seawalls are eligible to be on the National Register of Historic Places."

Carmen could feel Hugo's rush of confidence. Although they both knew it was only a matter of time before the entire waterfront would be developed, for now, knowing the developers of Pier 50 would have to wait for the City to determine if the seawall can take what's coming, it felt like a win.

"Gold Rush ships deliberately sunk to make those walls. How romantic can you get?" She looked at Hugo seductively.

"Nate would have certainly come in handy back then." That was the laugh they needed to take off the edge between them.

"Now Inspector, it's time to tell me what you really found under the pier."

No response.

"Tell me, Hugo," Carmen begged softly. "What did you find?"

"*My father*," he told her. It was the only way he could describe what it felt like to pull the little blue bottle from the seawall.

Hugo steered the BMW into a beautiful viewpoint to let memories of his father flood in, memories of how tired his father looked after a hard day on the docks. The estranged couple sat close to each other in silence.

"I think I understand what you were trying to tell me last night," Carmen began. "Grace falling to her death pushed Jack to the edge. Cate watching her son struggle for years pushed her to do something completely insane to save him," Carmen said wistfully.

Hugo's jaw was set. "I got the feeling Cate wanted to tell me everything, but I'm not sure she even knows the truth about what happened. Did she know if Jack cleared the meadow for the cannabis, or was hops to be the crop all along? Jack was lost to her, but not Nate. Cate told me over and over she wanted the ranch for her grandson, but she just kept saying, '*He's not mine.*' which makes me wonder that if she can even hold onto the ranch—would Nate stay?"

"Eli will do what he can," Carmen comforted.

Hugo let his mind drift a bit before pulling back onto the road. "I didn't dare ask her, but I think she knew since the day he was born that Jack wasn't the father."

Traffic on the coast was light that afternoon as they backtracked over their last ten miles. One or two cars passed on the ocean side heading south, but for the most part Hugo and Carmen had a stunning view of the water; it was intoxicating. They rode on in silence until Hugo turned down the long road to the lighthouse at Point Cabrillo, less than twenty miles shy of where they had started their journey at Chicken Cove.

"I promised Ava," is all Hugo would say.

The chop on the Pacific had calmed late in the day, allowing ribbons of blues and greens to reach beyond the horizon. Carmen and Hugo hiked out to the historic lighthouse where they had the full view of the coastline—no tourists, no official keepers, only fresh wrapped cookies left on the stoop should someone happen to pass by.

"I wonder how long we would last as lighthouse keepers?" speculated Carmen, enjoying a cookie as she leaned against the simple outpost.

"Hm?" As he wiped away a smudge of chocolate from her chin, he kissed her ever so lightly.

Unsettled by his own spontaneity, Hugo turned away and circled the lighthouse. On one of the turns, he saw his ex-wife reflected in the wavy glass of the antique windowpanes. Even with the added years, her form reminded Hugo of the young girl he had married. As if a schoolgirl playfully seeking her beau, Carmen rounded the tower in the other direction catching up to him at the signpost he was reading that told the story of the giant nineteenth-century Fresnel lens and how it signaled ships at sea.

"It's a bit garish, don't you agree? I mean, darling really, it's as if they pinched it from a dancehall," she teased and started to dance alone.

Of course, she was right. The giant lens did look like a mirror ball but was it was out of place? *What a splendid piece of engineering*, Hugo thought. *What a splendid woman*. He took her outstretched hand and they danced to the music of the waves, to the waterfall cry of a soaring hawk, to the rustle of birds in the dry chaparral.

Carmen pushed Hugo away. "Tell me honestly, does it feel strange *not* having the City under your feet; are you lost without *her*?"

Carmen had every right to be a jealous lover.

"It's only been seventy-two hours and I admit, it was strange at first not being on my turf," he confessed. "It's been absolutely wonderful seeing Ava and her whales. But to see a town fight so hard to survive, that alone—"

"—puts things into rather a harsh perspective, doesn't it?" Carmen finished his thought.

"Yes, yes it does. I slept like a baby the first night at the Inn, which surprised me." And then as he walked away before adding, "Last night, not so much. Also, a surprise."

Lured to the edge of the cliff by the rumble and crash of the surf, Carmen shouted over her shoulder, "Hugo, look! I see one!"

He raced to the cliff to pull Carmen away from the edge. Hugo was still shaking when he cradled her hand in his. It belonged there and he held onto it as they ran down the footpath that parted the rough beauty of the coast chaparral until they reached the crescent beach below the lighthouse.

The wash on the beach was filled with clues to the ocean's secrets: The arc of the last wave drawn by sinewy seaweed and broken shells, the thin crust of wet sand with breathing holes and in the backwater, clusters of goose barnacles clinging to the long leaves of the drifting kelp.

Fulfilling his promise to Ava, Hugo kicked off his shoes and emptied his pockets before wading into the untamed Pacific surf. Standing waist-deep, he scanned the open sea for the whale, Borsalino secured. It was the soft roar of the surf cresting over and over itself that reminded Hugo of the rhythmic changes in jazz. The harder he listened for the breaks, the more his body calmed in the cold waters, so quiet inside he could hear his father's reassuring voice, *"Keep your eyes on the horizon son, never turn your back."*

"Hugo," Carmen shouted from the shore. "Spouts!"

A mother gray whale had stationed herself just beyond the point, keeping her cyclopean eye on her offspring feeding in the shallows. Hugo could hear the *pouff* when the young gray whale surfaced from its dive after rolling along the rich muddy bottom of the North Coast sea.

EPILOGUE

THE NORTH COAST WAS A LONELY ONE. She was counting on it. If only she could get inside the kelp bed without colliding into the rocks, into the calm of the waters near the beach.

If only, then.

Land has a smell all its own. Some cities spew a stench of waste and greed as far as the horizon but on the North Coast, it was a less angry, even welcoming smell. It was all she could do to follow it away from the 178-foot, steel-hulled *Pacific Sea Scout* as the phantom ship split her sea in two. She struggled to keep her eyes open, steering toward the sound of the breakers as they crashed into the rocks. Her only hope was that a swell or a sneaker wave would carry her into a safe harbor.

The sea's pitch and roll guided her into shore, but not fast enough, as she was losing her strength with each agonizing kick of her tail. As she neared the coast, the alarms and shouts from the ship's deck faded before disappearing altogether, along with its useless beacon light; finally, its ominous silhouette was swallowed by jagged landforms to the south. She knew she was closing in on the beach, but it was painful to stay afloat. Unable to pilot herself to shore, she drifted helplessly toward the rocks.

"So close," she thought, sensing the land nearby.

Pouff. A pod of dolphins skirted the kelp. *Pouff.*

The sound of their breathing reminded her of her precious cargo. One more roll to the side in desperation to change her approach, but she was certain death would beat her to shore.

As she closed her eyes in defeat, the blue whale felt a gentle nudge near her tail, followed by another nudge, then another. The last contact came perilously close to the fatal gash just shy of her dorsal fin where the dispassionate hull of the unsuspecting research vessel had opened a hole in her side. Gentle nudges, but strong enough to keep her from the rocks and steer her into the cove.

It was a remarkable day. It was a day when the blue green Pacific cascaded into the bays and inlets of Mendocino's North Coast with spirited and unrestrained embrace. It was on that day a 600-pound sea lion pushed a 100,000-pound blue whale to shore, helping her ride the backs of the breakers to the sandy intertidal where she would give birth.

THE HUGO SANDOVAL ECO-MYSTERY SERIES

Take a peek at Hugo Sandoval's next investigation in Jann Eyrich's forthcoming mystery:

THE BLIND KEY

Coming Spring 2024

CHAPTER ONE

THE FOG BEDDED T. RAY HARRISON's red-eye on the tarmac at Dallas for nearly an hour after he changed planes.

"Traffic,"The captain's voice came across the speaker.

T. Ray was already on edge about the trip and the thought of jumping ship kept popping into his head. Add to his state of mind the memory of the rock-skipping landing at the lake two summers ago with Hugo and the girls, and he wondered if he would ever warm to flying ever again. He had been booked First Class which kept the Dewar's with the one large ice cube coming.

A cherry-faced blonde from Marfa, Texas, the flight attendant could see T. Ray was having trouble falling asleep and suggested movies in addition to the scotch to keep him company through the night. She had no way of knowing that the movie in his head beat out whatever the airline could possibly play on the tiny screen inches from the rough-edged investigator's nose.

T. Ray Harrison, III, San Francisco's forensic building inspector and special consultant to Otis Street, took advantage of the layover to confide in someone who was not his wife or Hugo. He dialed Hugo's office at the DBI, known as Otis Street, confident the call would be forwarded to Sara Dunne, Hugo's right hand. Despite the late hour, he expected Sara to pick up, and she did.

His opener was direct. "I gotta run something by you. Got a minute?"

Coming out of a deep sleep, she recognized the husky voice. But what confused her was that T. Ray was even on a plane, as she and the entire crew downtown knew the investigator had sworn off flying. Just hours before, T. Ray had delivered his report on the Dogpatch Project to Sara at Otis Street. While pointing out the clearances and permits required to move a Victorian-era three-story house eight blocks to a new housing development, he slipped in that he was headed home for a long weekend with his wife in Mendocino.

While the sleepy assistant listened to his explanation, she overheard the flight attendant in the background ask T. Ray if he wanted a refill. He did.

"All it took was one phone call and she put you on a plane? Who is this woman?" Sara whispered, hoping not to wake her sleeping kids.

"Marlena Sebastian Rincon," he began. "A Cuban cocktail, an islander just like Hugo, but more Afro-Cuban." T. Ray shook his icy drink at the word *cocktail*. "I thought I had left that part of my life behind, buried on some no-name beach. That is, until today, when a rogue wave took the sand away." He paused. "She was wild back then; still is, as far as I know."

"What time is it?" Sara was still not quite awake. T. Ray mumbled something she couldn't understand about time, no doubt something philosophical before returning to his confession.

"I never called her anything but Lena. She was a genuine reflection of Lena Horne, though her own eyes were crystal blue. My memory of her is intact." He laughed softly. "Polite to say her curves never straightened out." He sipped on his scotch while he dug into the complimentary late-night snack plate, his second.

Sara thought she could hear him smiling.

The PA on the plane announced, "We have been cleared for takeoff."

"You think she's on the level?"

"Well, I am on the plane, Sara. Trust me, this woman has always been charmed by the dramatic but calling me for kicks is not her style. She's a famous painter now. She wrote me out of her life long before my phone rang this morning, so whatever this is, I know it's real. We didn't have much of a conversation. In fact, you could say it wasn't a conversation at all, but it was enough to hear the fear in her voice. 'Meet Izzy at Marlowe's. Life or death'—her words— and then the line went dead."

Sara was sitting up in bed, her Notepad turned on.

"Twenty years and still that smokey voice hits me behind the knees. Hard."

"Where is this island, Harrison?" Sara wanted to scream, *Snap out of it!* There was a long pause on the other end. "I pulled up a map. Now what? Help me out, Harrison, where do I look?"

"It's near Captiva and Sanibel off the west coast of Florida out in the Gulf. Look for North Captiva and you should find it. Blind Key's not much of an island, just mangroves and oyster beds, a sandy shoal sticking out of the water. She's all alone on that coastline."

Sara wasn't sure if T. Ray was talking about the island or this woman.

"It's tough to find on a map," T. Ray said. "I get it. Hell, when you're on the water it's near impossible to see the key even if you're sailing straight for her."

"It's not on the map. I've found North Captiva but no Blind Key."

"Ah, she's there. A delicate flower; isolation in plain view."

"You sound like a poet, Harrison,"

"Do I? Well, five years of memories will do that to you, especially when they get dredged up out of the blue," he mused. "I thought I had left that life behind."

"Anything on this island?"

T. Ray muscled on. "It had been a plantation until the nineteen twenties: sugar cane, I think. Lena bought it with her first big commission in the '80s when money was flowing in. The island was a mess when I left but she was thinking she could tame it—like she tried to tame me."

It was all coming back to him—the soft winds, the taste of the Gulf air, Lena's curvy shadow on the perfect white sands. "Shellmound came with a big house and a handful of shacks, but not much else," said T. Ray, sounding nearly sober.

"Shellmound?"

"Yeah, that was the name of the plantation on Blind Key. Unless the hurricanes have taken over and Lena is living in a double-wide, the big house should still be standing."

"Does this eccentric artist live out there alone?"

"No idea. Marlowe is her husband; at least he used to be. Can't be sure how they're getting on, especially since she called me," said T. Ray, flagging the attendant for a refill before wheels up.

"And you think it's the brother she's worried about."

"Baby brother. Gotta be. Last I heard from him was about ten years ago. He called for money. Paid it back. I didn't want to know why at the time, but I found out later he was in over his head back then, running Cubans to Miami; his own freedom train." T. Ray stopped to remember the kid. "Israel; Izzy. Good heart. He used to live in the boathouse on the island. Lena used to paint there. Maybe she still does."

Sara was wide awake, her fluid mind running a mile a minute. She wondered what could make this Lena so desperate that she would bring her old lover back into her life? And whose life was really in danger—hers or her brother's? Sara was worried. T. Ray was a man of his word but it was starting to sound to her like somewhere over Texas he had started to question his decision to rescue this woman. And he had lied to Daisy on top of that.

"Sara, it's not so much about not being completely honest with Daisy that bothers me. It's what I might be getting Hugo into."

"'You know I wouldn't call you if I had any other choice,' she said to me, just like that." T. Ray recounted. "Then she asked me was I still digging around for that building inspector? I gotta say that threw me, especially when she didn't wait to hear my answer. Sara, it was as if she already knew about me and Hugo. It's a bit disturbing."

Sara found it surprising as well.

"Finally, Lena spit out the flight number and ended the call with the plea, *meet me at Marlowe's, life or death.*"

The attendant whispered in passing, "You need to put your phone on airplane mode now."

"What do you want me to tell the chief? Harrison? T. Ray, you still there?"

His voice came through at last. "Hold off on that, would ya, darlin'? Not a peep. I'll be in touch."

Then dead air.

Enjoy more about

The Rotting Whale

Meet the Author

Check out author appearances

Explore special features

ABOUT THE AUTHOR

JANN EYRICH was born and raised in Cincinnati — although the writer claims her spiritual roots are tethered to rural Northern Michigan. After setting anchor in San Francisco, she has roamed from LA to New York, working in film and touring art exhibits. Extensive trips to the Four Corners region followed by an Orion retreat in "The Kingdom" of Vermont sealed Eyrich's passion for environmental writers and their voices.

Trained as a documentary filmmaker, the author has written eco-themed screenplays and short stories which led to this current book series reflecting the collision of nature with the built environment.

Working as a hands-on, independent woman contractor in San Francisco for twenty years, Eyrich resided in the legendary shacks of Telegraph Hill where the writer was gifted anchorage to the City, along with insight into the lives of the characters she continues to create.

Today, she writes from her home in Northern California where she feeds the project's website - **hugomysteries.com** - with current news of interest to Hugo on the ecopolitical fronts inside San Francisco and wherever he ventures outside his City's limits.

ACKNOWLEDGEMENTS

I would like to acknowledge two points of inspiration that have made indelible marks on this book. First was the afternoon on a catwalk when I peered into the mudflats of the San Pablo Bay for hours watching the life in the slough come and go on the tide; years later it was the moment when I walked through the open barn doors of the Folsom Street blacksmith shop, its dark interior on that rare sun-bleached day revealing a secret portal into the City. These two experiences are inexorably linked and together anchor these pages.

Twenty years in the City; twenty years gone. Truth is I never left San Francisco, not entirely. In those years I lived in the graces of a legendary couple, Valetta and Desmond Heslet, who did far more than share their remarkable view from their cottage on Telegraph Hill; they shared their stories from their long history in North Beach.

Now that I'm talking stories, I owe a huge debt to my friend Tony Rosellini whose conversations in the open doorway to his blacksmith shop or at the smithy's annual Christmas parties introduced me to a unique layer of the City and the people in it.

For all the adventures leading to this book, I'd like to thank Shawn Hall who unselfishly created a space in each of her design + build projects for my writing. With her environmental sensibilities, Shawn proves to be an invaluable editor for Hugo's eco-mysteries.

I have been deeply inspired by the town of Fort Bragg, a town that refuses to live apart from the sea. In 2009, citizens of this coastal community took in a stranded blue whale which they have passionately turned into their future. Cheers to the birth of the Noyo Center for Marine Science and the over 200 people who "saved" a skeleton.

No small thanks go to my publisher Vicki DeArmon, my editor, Julia Park Tracey and all the team at Sibylline Press. I am proud to be represented by you and I want to thank you for faith in this book.

From the early drafts on, I owe a huge debt of gratitude to all my readers. This is a courageous bunch including Teri Ketchie, Carole Sieving, Shawn Hall, Dianne Tanner, Jane Koppenhoefer, Toni Eyrich, Margaret Curtis, Dave Eyrich, Marc Curtis, Mary Pecka, Rob Scheid, Lee Leibrock, Hazel Meier, Daniel Meier, Mike Sieving, Barbara Paulson, Margo Merck, David Jenkins, MaryAlice Duhme, Sharon Connor, Meriku Lewis, Amie Hall, Nancy Williams, Debbie Cundall, Talitha Wesson, and George Henshaw. I fear I may have missed someone; if so, my apologies.

Without a doubt, it has been my family that has kept me footed with their encouragement and support. I tell these stories for them. Never lost, never alone.

And finally, this book is dedicated to those who fight to slow down the ships and create safe corridors for whales. In the increasingly busy shipping lanes, it is the blue whale off our Pacific shores and the North Atlantic right whale which today are destined for extinction, unless...

Sibylline Press is proud to publish the brilliant work of women authors over 50. We are a woman-owned publishing company and, like our authors, represent women of a certain age. In our first season we have three outstanding fiction (historical fiction and mystery) and three incredible memoirs to share with readers of all ages.

HISTORICAL FICTION

The Bereaved: A Novel

BY JULIA PARK TRACEY

Paperback ISBN: 978-1-7367954-2-2
5 3/8 x 8 3/4 | 274 pages | $18
ePub ISBN: 978-1-9605730-0-1 | $12.60

Based on the author's research into her grandfather's past as an adopted child, and the surprising discovery of his family of origin and how he came to be adopted, Julia Park Tracey has created a mesmerizing work of historical fiction illuminating the darkest side of the Orphan Train.

Unsettled: A Novel

BY PATRICIA REIS

Paperback ISBN: 978-1-7367954-8-4
5 3/8 x 8 3/4 | 378 pages | $19
ePUB ISBN: 978-1-960573-05-6 | $13.30

In this lyrical historical fiction with alternating points of view, a repressed woman begins an ancestral quest through the prairies of Iowa, awakening family secrets and herself, while in the late 1800s, a repressed ancestor, Tante Kate, creates those secrets.

MYSTERY

The Rotting Whale: A Hugo Sandoval Eco-Mystery

By Jann Eyrich

Paperback ISBN: 978-1-7367954-3-9
5 3/8 x 8 3/8 | 212 pages | $17
ePub ISBN: 978-1-960573-03-2 | $11.90

In this first case in the new Hugo Sandoval Eco-Mystery series, an old-school San Francisco building inspector with his trademark Borsalino fedora, must reluctantly venture outside his beloved city and find his sea legs before he can solve the mystery of how a 90-ton blue whale became stranded, twice, in a remote inlet off the North Coast.

More titles in this eco-mystery series to come:
Spring '24: ***The Blind Key*** | ISBN: 978-1-7367954-5-3
Fall '24: ***The Singing Lighthouse*** | ISBN: 978-1-7367954-6-0

MEMOIR

These Broken Roads: Scammed and Vindicated, One Woman's Story

By Donna Marie Hayes

Tradepaper ISBN: 978-1-7367954-4-6
5 3/8 x 8 3/8 | 226 pages | $17
ePUB ISBN: 978-1-960573-04-9 | $11.90

In this gripping and honest memoir, Jamaican immigrant Donna Marie Hayes recounts how at the peak of her American success in New York City, she is scammed and robbed of her life's savings by the "love of her life" met on an online dating site and how she vindicates herself to overcome a lifetime of bad choices.

MEMOIR *(cont.)*

Maeve Rising: Coming Out Trans in Corporate America

By Maeve DuVally

Paperback ISBN: 978-1-7367954-1-5
5 3/8 x 8 3/8 | 284 pages | $18
ePub ISBN: 978-1-960573-01-8 | $12.60

In this searingly honest LBGQT+ memoir, Maeve DuVally tells the story of coming out transgender in one of the most high-profile financial institutions in America, Goldman Sachs.

Reading Jane: A Daughter's Memoir

By Susannah Kennedy

Paperback ISBN: 978-1-7367954-7-7
5 3/8 x 8 3/8 | 306 pages | $19
ePub ISBN: 978-1-960573-02-5 | $13.30

After the calculated suicide of her domineering and narcissistic mother, Susannah Kennedy grapples with the ties between mothers and daughters and the choices parents make in this gripping memoir that shows what freedom looks like when we choose to examine the uncomfortable past.

For more information about Sibylline Press and our authors, please visit us at **www.sibyllinepress.com**